The Park

The Park is a tale of terror in the city. It is
all the more frightening because it *could*
happen here. Maybe it already has.

It is a hot summer in Manhattan, and
Central Park is alive with mimes, vendors,
tourists, mothers-with-toddlers, drug-ped-
dlers, softball players, and a psychopathic
killer.

The killer's first victim is fifteen-year-old
Chico Torres. The police find him lying on
the grass and think he is asleep. When
they get closer, they see the perfect red
circle of blood on his chest, right over his
heart.

Soon there are other victims, all teen-
agers, all boys. The few clues the police
unearth lead nowhere, and Warren Jackson, a black undercover policeman, is assigned to the case. Using a few shreds of
evidence, Jackson tries to reconstruct the
kind of person who could have perpetra-

(continued on back flap)

ALSO BY DON GOLD

Bellevue
Letters to Tracy

(continued from front flap)

ted the crimes. He realizes that only by
using another likely victim as a decoy will
he be able to trap the lonely, desperate
character who passes all but unnoticed
through the many worlds that co-exist in
the park.

The Park

A novel by
Don Gold

HARPER & ROW, PUBLISHERS

NEW YORK, HAGERSTOWN, SAN FRANCISCO, LONDON

To my mother and my father

In such a park, the citizens who would take excursions in carriages, or on horseback, could have the substantial delights of country roads and country scenery, and forget for a time the rattle of the pavements and the glare of brick walls. Pedestrians would find quiet and secluded walks when they wished to be solitary, and broad alleys filled with thousands of happy faces, when they would be gay. The thoughtful denizen of the town would go out there in the morning to hold converse with the whispering trees, and the wearied tradesmen in the evening, to enjoy an hour of happiness by mingling in the open spaces with "all the world."

—Andrew Jackson Downing
The Horticulturist, 1851

All classes represented with a common purpose, not at all intellectual, competitive with none, disposing to jealousy and spiritual or intellectual pride toward none, each individual adding by his mere presence to the pleasure of all others; all helping to the greater happiness of each. You may thus often see vast numbers of persons brought closely together, poor and rich, young and old, Jew and Gentile. . . . Is it doubtful that it does men good to come together in this way in pure air and under the light of heaven?

—Frederick Law Olmsted

Of all the city's wonders, Central Park ranks first in the affection of New Yorkers. Hundreds of thousands think of it as "their park." Twelve million wander through it yearly, making it the most heavily frequented park of its size in the world. The park is many things to many people.

—Henry Hope Reed
*Central Park: A History
and a Guide*

Wednesday

Chico Torres awoke at ten A.M. in a silent apartment. His mother had gone to her job in the garment center; his father had not been home in days. There was a large box of Captain Crunch cereal on the kitchen table. Chico swiped at two roaches that were attempting to invade the box, sending them scurrying, took a chipped bowl from a cabinet and filled it. He got a carton of milk from the refrigerator and poured some over the cereal. He ate slowly.

He had been out past midnight with Rodriguez and Martinez. They had walked for blocks, making small talk, joking, staring at girls. Then Martinez suggested that they hit the yards. Although it was a warm night, they had all worn jackets, so the cans of spray paint would not be visible. At the 242nd Street yards they had dodged laborers and Transit Authority police successfully until the last minute, when they were spotted. Each of them ran in a different direction. Chico vaulted a low fence, dashed along the tracks and emerged through a street grating on the upper west side. Feeling triumphant—he had managed one large CHEETAH 101 on the side of a number "1" train—he boarded a bus heading crosstown and had arrived at home in East Harlem at twelve-thirty. His mother was asleep, so he did not make any noise; he headed for his room, put the paint can beneath a pile of shirts in a drawer and went to sleep.

3

As he munched the cereal, he thought about the fate of the others. He was confident that none had been arrested. They could run, as he could, and it had happened before and they'd all gotten away. Even if they had been caught, it would have meant no more than a confrontation with an angry mother summoned to the station for a lecture by the local police youth officer. At age fifteen, Chico realized that he was still categorized as a juvenile; next year, at sixteen, it would be a different matter; and his inherent sense of caution led him to conclude that it would be wise to abandon writing on that significant birthday.

He finished the cereal, looked in the refrigerator for something else to eat and saw nothing that interested him. He slammed the refrigerator door and went back to his room. He put on his battered sneakers, a pair of torn and paint-stained jeans and a Rolling Stones T-shirt. He went to the phone and called Rodriguez. "What are you doin'?"

"Nothin'," Rodriguez answered.

"What happened last night?"

"We made it. Man, them cops is slow."

"Beautiful. What you doin' today?"

"I don't know. Maybe I'll see you later in the park."

"Cool. I'll be around. Later."

Chico left the apartment and walked down upper Park Avenue. It was a quiet, hot day in the middle of summer. Without school to worry about, Chico was free to make his own decisions about where to go, what to eat, who to see; his mother worried less about him during the summer, or at least she seemed to be less interested in lecturing him about his school work and his future. He felt free.

He cut across at 96th Street and walked over to Fifth Avenue. He felt the warmth of the sun and a layer of perspiration building up under his T-shirt. At Fifth he waited for a bus, and when one pulled up he waited again, for the rear door to open. Someone emerged, and Chico held the door open and leaped onto the bus; the driver didn't see him. In his pocket Chico could feel fifty cents; it would have to pay his way through the day.

He got off the bus at 72nd Street and entered the park. It was not as crowded as it would be on a weekend, but there were, apparently, many people who didn't have jobs to go to during the summer. He thought about it briefly, inconclusively, and forgot it. He strolled through the park, heading south. Two men walked past hand in hand. "Faggots," Chico's friends called them, spewing out the word as if cursing an enemy. Chico turned his head and smiled. Several women pushed baby carriages past him, and an old woman, her shopping bag beside her, was asleep on a bench. Chico looked around for one of his friends but did not see anyone he knew. He kept walking.

Edmund Wilton had hung up the OUT TO LUNCH sign, locked the gallery door and gone to Les Pleiades for lunch. He went there often, although he was aware of the fact that the staff treated him with less deference than they did the other gallery owners, the conspicuously successful ones whose names appeared in the paper, who bought large ads in the Sunday *Times.* He ate alone, as usual, and read the *Times,* which he bought on his way to the gallery in the morning and saved to enjoy over lunch.

Today he felt profoundly empty and depressed, a feeling that troubled him more and more lately. He wondered if it showed, if the others dining at the restaurant felt any pity for him. He remembered having lunch once at La Côte Basque and seeing Alec Guinness eating alone, reading a book, and feeling that such a great man should not be without companionship. The emptiness he felt must be loneliness, he realized.

He ate and glanced through the *Times.* There was a story about an art fraud that intrigued him momentarily, before his thoughts brought him to the conclusion that he was committing fraud almost every day when he sold an inferior painting at an inflated price. He turned the page and saw a story about decreasing crime in Central Park. He spent days of his life in the park, walking his

5

dog, and he had rarely felt a twinge of fear, but the story, designed to comfort the reader, only served to annoy him, to remind him of the dangers that were said to exist in the park. What could he do about them? he thought. Nothing. He would not wear old clothes; he would not seem pathetic in order to appear to be invisible, immune to the threats of the criminals who found profit in the park. He might stay out of the park after sundown. He had not lingered much longer than that in the past, but now he would try to bring his dog home before darkness fell.

He finished his lunch and the *Times,* paid his check, left his customary 15 per cent tip—the waiter never said thank you—and walked out into the sunlight. He walked over to his apartment and got Bernard, his chow, who barked happily when he entered. He slipped his arm through the strap of his shoulder bag, attached the leash to Bernard's collar and went out, heading for the park. He felt like a walk, and business was slow at the gallery, so he did not feel guilty about leaving the gallery closed.

Bernard pulled at the leash enthusiastically. Together they entered the park at 72nd Street.

Chico was restless. He had checked out the band shell for any of his friends and had not found anyone he knew. A tall black man had offered to sell him some LSD or mescaline, but when Chico pulled the two quarters out of his pocket, the pusher had laughed and moved on.

He thought about going home and watching television until a friend called, but it was a pleasant summer day and he didn't want to waste it by staying in the apartment. He sat down on a small knoll of grass on the eastern side of the mall, put his head down and felt drowsy.

He heard a dog bark softly, and he sat up.

Wilton was numb, and when he looked around he couldn't hear anything, as if the park had become the setting for a silent film. It was not until he had taken Bernard back to the apartment that he realized that he had sweated profusely through his shirt. He took a shower, and as he did he felt the numbness slowly fade. He thought that he might be acquiring a circulatory disorder, something he would have to mention to his doctor at his next check-up. The vague pain in his eyes that he had felt in the park vanished too. He changed shirts, put a bit of food out for Bernard and went back to the gallery.

He sat behind his desk staring at a Picasso lithograph he did not want to sell. He thought he remembered meeting a boy in the park. He had tried to be friendly to the boy, but something had gone wrong. Too bad, he thought. On the other hand, if they met again in the park, perhaps some kind of friendship could grow.

A customer came into the gallery and he moved forward to greet her.

Thursday

The Central Park police precinct house sits like a squat old fortress soiled by the winds of decades and the grit of the city. Its reddish-brown brick and stone face hugs the park's transverse road midway along the road from the 86th Street entrance on Central Park West to where 84th Street and Fifth Avenue meet, beside the Metropolitan Museum of Art. It is a nineteenth-century complex, a leftover from the days when Olmsted and Vaux saw the park take shape. It was an arsenal during part of its history and also a stable before the police took it over. It houses 125 members of the force during their shifts, and its adjoining parking lot is a line-up of their vehicles. It has a single cell. Prisoners are not kept long; they are shipped on.

For the members of the force who man the precinct it is, clearly, pastoral duty compared to any other precinct in Manhattan. Most of them learn quickly that the pastoral quality is deceiving. It does not mean "peaceful." For Sergeant Fahey it could, on bad days, resemble chaos.

This had not been a good week for Fahey. He sat behind his desk in his cramped office and glared at the peeling walls and aged furniture around him. Normally he would not have paid attention to them; they had become a part of his daily life. Today he noticed them, and he knew why.

His wife had been cheerless for days, and he hadn't had time to find out what was bothering her. His son, at fourteen, was spending too much time outside of their apartment; Fahey would have to talk to him as well very soon. These thoughts nagged at him, dancing around the edge of the problems he faced on his job.

This week a sixty-year-old man had been attacked by two gunmen near the boat house on the edge of the lake. They had attempted to seize his wallet; there had been a struggle. The man managed to save his money, but one of the gunmen, frustrated, had taken a shot at him, wounding him in the leg. The gunmen escaped. It had happened before, that sort of episode, but in this case the newspapers had sent out reporters to interview the victim. He had said—and Fahey had read it in three different papers —"It is a terrifying thing. You can't even walk in Central Park anymore."

The Captain had called him in after that one.

"Do you know what this means?" he had asked Fahey. "It means, and don't forget it, that we're not doing our job. Whether we are or not, whether we think we are or not, that's what the hell it means. If we catch those two bastards, it won't matter. That'll be buried somewhere in the same papers. What has been printed is what makes it tough for us."

Fahey complained that he had no control over what respectable citizens, assaulted in the park, told the press. He had helped get the guy to a hospital and set up the search for the gunmen; that was all he could do, he protested.

The Captain puffed on his cigar vigorously, looking as if he might devour it, and didn't respond.

That was one of several troubling moments this week. The Haitians had staged another of their lunatic voodoo rites at the north end of the park and when one of Fahey's men had come upon it—complete with chicken blood and moaning—he was belted by one of the Haitians. Then there was the report from the new man, Harrigan, who recited without a smile that a horse had been hijacked.

"This guy jumps out of the bushes, pushes the woman off the goddamned horse, mounts it and races away on it," Harrigan had said.

"Well, he can't hide the fucking horse," Fahey had told him, "and he's not about to hold it hostage for ransom."

Fahey had instructed Harrigan to find both horse and rider, before the woman issued a statement to the press about how tough it was to ride a horse in Central Park. Harrigan found the horse, riderless, and Fahey considered that to be a stand-off.

But the worst was to come. One of his men, Albert Martin, had been on routine patrol near the band shell. He rushed into Fahey's office, his shirt stained with sweat, a grimace on his face.

"It was like this," Martin told Fahey. "I was walking, just walking, nothing happening. The usual. A couple trying to make it. A kid smoking a joint. I told him to cool it. He looked about twelve. A guy playing with himself. I told him to go home and play. Then I saw this kid on the grass. I thought he was asleep. I wasn't going to do anything, actually, but I walked over just to take a look. A kid about fifteen. I thought he was asleep. I tapped him with my shoe, and he didn't move. I leaned over and looked at his T-shirt, and it wasn't a design I saw. Blood, in a perfect red circle on his chest, right over his heart. Blood. That's when I got help. The kid was dead. Shot. So I got help, like you always say to do."

Through an expired student bus pass in his wallet, the boy was identified as Chico Torres, with an upper east side address. Fahey found the phone number and called it. No answer. He told Martin to move on, to get back to his beat. Fahey stared into space. Then he made several phone calls to neighbors of Torres and from one of them got the mother's phone number at work. He got through to her.

The depressing conversation was all too familiar to Fahey. He had made many such calls before. The mother, on the edge of hysteria when Fahey began by identifying himself, became totally hysterical by the end of it. She would come right down to the Central Park station, after identifying the body.

When she arrived, she seemed too weak to talk.

Fahey recited his questions, staring at her constantly.

"Did Chico have any enemies? Someone with whom he had a fight lately?"

"No."

She said that Chico was a good boy and that his father didn't do much to help her raise Chico and that she had done the best she could do.

"I believe you," Fahey said.

"Tell me what happened?" she asked.

"We don't know. One of our men was on duty and he walked past your son, who he thought was sleeping, but when he poked him to get him up he realized that the boy wasn't asleep. He'd been shot, once."

"Madre de Dios," she said softly, and wept.

Fahey asked one of his men to drive her home. The Medical Examiner would have a report, he knew, and that might tell him something. When the report came in, it did tell him something, but not enough. The boy had been killed with a single shot from a .22 caliber weapon. According to the ME, the gun had been held directly against the boy's chest, at his heart. There had been powder residue and shavings of lead from the slug inside the wound.

It was almost useless information. Someone had killed the boy, motive undetermined; that was all that Fahey could conclude.

Today at his tattered, cluttered desk it was the one case he thought about while all his other frustrations competed for attention. He stood up to stretch. Tall and still thin after twenty years on the force, he wondered why his hair hadn't turned gray. Miraculously it had remained black through it all, through the years on a beat, through the occasions when he'd been shot at

14

(and wounded three times), through the moments when he had managed to shoot first at that split second when such a decision must be made wisely, and now, through the day-after-day rituals and puzzles of life in Central Park.

He walked out of his office and stopped a passing detective, Waterman. "Got anything on Torres?" he asked.

"Nothing," Waterman grunted.

Like a surgeon who feels worse when he loses a young patient, Fahey was troubled by this case. The old ones are closer to death anyway, he felt; the young ones are the saddest cases.

"What do you figure on doing?" he wanted to know.

"Look. And look some more. What can we do? Everybody knows what happened to Torres, but nobody knows how it happened. So we really don't know what we're looking for. Another kid? A pusher? We can't find any record of drug use with this kid. A lunatic? My God, there are enough of those around. Ballistics has given us a bit on the gun, and we've got the slug. So what? The guy who owns the gun hasn't been in touch."

"Well, we can try to find out more about the kid, right? Who he knew."

"Sure. And we will. But I've got the feeling we won't find much. I talked to the kid's mother, too. They all say their kids are good kids, but this one I believe. Great. Now what do we do? I can't put on jeans and a T-shirt and sit in the park and wait. I don't look the part, and we haven't any teen-agers on the force these days."

"I know, I know"—Fahey nodded—"but you never know about kids. Mine is fourteen, and I'm not always sure what he's into."

"Don't worry about your kid. Let me worry about Torres, and we'll see what happens."

"Meanwhile the *Times* and the *News* and the *Post* and God knows who else will be digging into it."

"Let them dig. If they find out something we haven't found out, I'll be happy to get it."

"Wonderful. First that old guy gets attacked and screams that Central Park isn't safe for anyone, now we've got a dead kid and no motive and no weapon and no suspect and we're pretending that we know what we're doing."

"We're not pretending. We know. Give us some time and we'll have something for you. I promise."

"You promise." Fahey sighed.

Waterman walked out into the heat of the summer day. Fahey had almost forgotten that it was summer until he felt wet beneath his arms.

At that moment a well-dressed middle-aged woman strode through the door. She spotted Fahey.

"I have lived on Fifth Avenue for twenty-five years," she shouted. "I remember when the neighborhood was a peaceful place, when I was proud to be able to live in it."

"Can I help you?" Fahey asked.

"You can help all of us," she snapped.

"How?"

"By catching him."

"By catching him?"

"Yes. It was awful. I had left my apartment and I was walking alongside the park on Fifth, as I often do. It is a lovely walk, even now, even with all these things going on."

"And what happened?"

"A man came climbing over the wall and leaped down a few feet in front of me."

"What did he do?"

"He didn't *do* anything. He just stopped there and stared at me. His eyes were wild."

"And then?"

"And then nothing."

"What are you trying to tell me?" Fahey asked.

"Well, he was naked. Absolutely naked. And after he stopped there to look at me, he just went walking along as calmly as if he were in the Easter Parade. It was absolutely disgusting."

16

"Don't worry. Nobody walks around naked for long."

"I certainly hope not," the woman said, trembling.

"You just go home and relax, and without a doubt one of our men will be bringing him in soon." He escorted her to the door.

A few minutes later two of his men walked in flanking a naked man.

"Why? Why?" Fahey asked the man, who was in his twenties, short, chubby, with long hair in a ponytail.

"Hot, man," the nudist said. "Very hot out there."

"You on something?" Fahey asked.

"Maybe. A little acid. Not more than that. Who are you?"

"A friend," Fahey said wearily. "Get him something to wear," he added to the men grasping the exhibitionist. "And get him down to Bellevue."

Fahey plunged his hands into his pockets. He could feel the sweat dripping down his forehead. He walked outside. It was hot. He stared at the people strolling by. More than usual for a weekday, he thought, as if it were a footnote to everything that had bothered him this week. But he knew it would be worse on the weekend, when everyone who didn't own an air conditioner would seek out a cool spot in the park, despite the fact that such cool spots really didn't exist. He knew from experience that crowds bred more trouble, for themselves, for him, for the precinct.

One of his better young men, Mark Goldman, walked up to Fahey. He was on a break from foot patrol near the precinct house.

"I heard," Goldman said. "About the kid."

"Yeah," Fahey grunted.

"Can we get any help on this one?" Goldman asked.

"Who knows? The city is saving money everywhere. We haven't got enough guys to do what we ought to be doing. Homicide will be out there, with its suits and ties, asking questions nobody can answer. The few guys I can spare will hide in the bushes or pretend to be asleep on benches or just out there looking zonked and harmless. You know what happens in this town when you get what looks like a clever killer working you over? Everybody says they want to get involved. You get the Area Command interested and Homicide and the Detective Bureau's intelligence unit and the major case section of the Special Investigations Division and our own Anti-Crime Unit and guys like you in good old blue pounding the turf with their eyes open. And it's all not enough. We haven't got enough guys right here where we need them."

"What about the Street Crime Unit?" Goldman asked.

"I'll talk to the Captain about it," Fahey replied.

"Which means what?"

"Which means that if the Captain chooses to ask for one of their men we'll get one of their men."

"Do you think he should ask?"

"Of course I think he should ask. I need anybody I can get on this one."

"Ask for Jackson," Goldman suggested.

"Who the hell is Jackson?" Fahey snapped.

"An old friend of mine and a good cop. Black. Smart. Careful."

"Fine, I'll tell the Captain to order black, smart, careful Jackson."

"When?"

"Very soon."

Goldman went back on patrol and Fahey returned to his current obsession. Who killed Torres? he asked himself. And why?

The lack of any answers annoyed him. He went back into the station house and saw the nudist, now in a pair of old pants and a soiled white T-shirt, between the two men who had brought him in.

"Take that son of a bitch to Bellevue. Now!" Fahey screamed.

The threesome ran for the door, and Fahey went into the Captain's office. "We need help on this one, on the Torres case," he said without an introduction. He didn't need one.

"I know," the Captain said. "I know."

"I've got a suggestion," Fahey said.

"I'll take your suggestion," the Captain responded.

Sunday

This had begun as a troubling day. Wilton had wanted to wear his Gucci loafers, but when he looked at them one shoe had a spot of mud on it. He couldn't rub it off. He grumbled to himself about it over a breakfast of gently scrambled eggs and broiled kippers. He had planned to wear those loafers, along with his new beige Daks trousers and the dark brown shirt he had bought at Bergdorf's. Now he couldn't do that. He thought about it, fretted and hissed, from nine A.M. until after eleven, when he concluded that his furry red dog, Bernard, needed walking. So he dressed as planned, but with another pair of shoes, softly gleaming dark brown boots from Lefcourt, a discovery he had made while walking along Madison Avenue one Saturday. A bargain, he had concluded, at $110.

He washed the dishes slowly and carefully and placed them precisely in a rack to dry. He put on his sunglasses and locked the door to his apartment. The dog tugged on the leash as they left the building on 72nd Street between Fifth and Madison, a few steps from the park. The doorman bowed subserviently and chanted, "Good morning."

As he walked toward the park, he realized that he had taken his new shoulder bag, a small polished leather bag on a strap. It slapped gently against his side as he walked. He did not remember removing it from the drawer. That was a problem he had been having in recent weeks: mailing letters and forgetting if he had mailed them, paying bills and forgetting if he had paid them. He had gone to the model-soldier store on Madison Avenue and had bought a rare and beautiful eighteenth-century French soldier for his collection; when he got home he discovered that he already owned such a soldier. He suffered the duplication, although when he saw the two side by side the sight offended him.

The light turned green and the chow lurched forward as if he understood the color. The dog was smart, but he kept his perceptions and his knowledge hidden, to be revealed in odd and sudden ways. He was a moody animal, given to hours of seemingly brooding isolation, difficult to love but handsome enough, his owner felt, to appreciate, the way a child appreciates a large stuffed animal.

They lived together, man and dog, with few intrusions. An ideal arrangement, the man thought as the two entered the park. No one to be strident about his unwillingness to get out of bed in the morning. No one to be sloppy, to cook badly. He thought of his marriage, years ago, a marriage that lasted just two months. They had barely touched before the wedding, and when he did so, hesitantly, on their first night together, she had said that she felt violated. He withdrew. They had laughed together and played together, but that was not enough. They parted solemnly, and he concluded that he did not need women and was not in need of men either. His business and his privacy and his dog were sufficient, he thought, remembering belatedly that his psychiatrist mattered to him too. Their sessions brought him some sense of identity, of comprehension, although there were matters that they did not seem to include in their conversation.

He saw himself, a man in his fifties, as a dapper contemporary version of Clifton Webb, but in better shape physically and certainly not effeminate. But when he chose to mention that similarity to others, and that didn't happen often, he would have to ask if they had ever seen the film *Laura,* and if they hadn't, he would feel foolish trying to describe Webb. It was a comparison he had considered abandoning; he thought about updating it.

In the gallery he owned, such comparisons were not necessary. He was known in the art world, not because his gallery was a prominent one, but because it had been a modestly successful one for years. He stocked it with inferior works by superior artists, many of which he selected on his annual trip to Europe. Most buyers, he knew, would not know where to find a first-rate Miró; he had second-rate ones and a suave way of describing them as first-rate. He had his clientele, and he had sustained its loyalty to him in the course of his conservative, sensible career.

If he worried at all, it was about robbery. There was much of it in New York, he realized, and reading the *Times* each day often made him anxious. Robbers were becoming more and more bold; a gallery down the street from his had been robbed at gunpoint in midday. He had found a small gun in a seedy midtown shop one day and had bought it, along with several rounds of ammunition. He had put it in a drawer and left it untouched for months. One evening he picked it up admiringly and thought that, if pressed, he might use it to defend his property. He did not see himself as a violent man, and the gun always seemed foreign in his hand. The noise it might make bothered him as well, and when he mentioned that, idly, to the building superintendent at the gallery, the man offered to construct a silencer for it, almost as a joke. He had accepted the offer.

But it was a lovely summer day and he didn't want to think about that now. The dog plunged on ahead of him, and he followed into the park.

He paused at the edge of the Great Lawn, west of the Metropolitan Museum, where he watched two Puerto Rican softball teams engaged in combat: Puente's Travel Agency versus Santamaria's Tavern. Between innings, dozens of cans of beer were plucked from a large bucket filled with ice. He saw four men, obviously foreign, approach the diamond. He eavesdropped as one of the men moved toward one of the Puerto Rican coaches.

25

"The lines, the white lines. What do they mean?" the man, speaking with a French accent, asked the coach.

"I ain't got no time now," the coach responded. The four Frenchmen smiled politely and meandered across the field. He watched them and laughed softly. He didn't understand softball, but he did understand that sort of confrontation, he thought.

He began to walk again, and in a few minutes was moving through the Ramble, between the lake and the 79th Street transverse. It was the closest thing to a jungle to be found in the park, thickly overgrown, and he didn't want to linger. Passersby had been attacked by muggers hiding in the bushes.

He saw two men slowly walking toward him. He recognized one of them, a married man who, with his wife, lived in his building. They had always seemed happy together. Suddenly the two men moved into the bushes and vanished.

Does his wife know? he thought, slightly troubled by the awareness that the brief episode had provided. He realized that he didn't care. He had little interest in homosexuals; when he did think about them at all, he wondered how they could duplicate the affection women provided.

He kept walking. He got to the Sheep Meadow, a sprawling expanse of lawn ringed by sidewalks, and stopped to survey the scene. He remembered reading somewhere that there had been sheep grazing on that grass until the 1930s. He couldn't recall where he had read it; it was not the sort of information he normally retained, not the sort he would pass along in conversation.

Several small boys were flying kites. He had done that as a boy too. Beside a large rock two lovers were attempting to do fully clothed what usually requires disrobing. He was offended by their boldness. Three dogs raced across the vast field, chasing each other or illusory enemies. Bernard tugged to join them.

He moved on. Time passed, but he barely realized it. In the small lake beneath the Belvedere Castle, two lonely swans glided across the water. He remembered hearing that the first swans in the park were a gift from the city of Hamburg. Nine out of twelve

26

succumbed to apoplexy, he recalled. "Ah, New York," he said aloud, then turned to see if anyone had heard him. No one had.

A few children, uninterested in swans, fished aimlessly in the lake, catching nothing. He watched them. Two teen-age boys were attempting to climb up the cliff below the castle, hoping, no doubt, to break into it. He wanted to tell them that the castle was empty; it held weather monitoring equipment, no more than that.

A group of drably dressed Russian mothers passed by pushing their babies in carriages, babbling in their mother tongue. A jogger in sweat suit passed, and he thought he recognized him, a well-known author whose name he could not summon. A majestically dressed black man in gleaming boots and jodhpurs—a pimp, he thought—was on a horse moving rapidly along the bridle path. A middle-aged stocky woman in slacks and sturdy shoes, clutching a birding guide, led six of her disciples past him. He could hear her reciting entries for her log: "Blue jay, sparrow hawk, downy woodpecker, English sparrow, starling, cardinal." And pigeon, he thought.

He headed toward the mall. Perhaps today, he thought, he would find someone to talk to, casually and productively. He did not truly search for companions, but lately he had wanted to talk, seriously, to someone other than his doctor. He had chatted for a few moments on Wednesday with a teen-age boy. It had come to nothing; the boy was not bright, not eager to talk, almost hostile. His own reaction had been close to anger, but he didn't remember displaying it.

In fact, as Bernard led him along the mall toward the band shell, he could not remember much about that encounter. There was something numbing about it, and he recalled with difficulty that he had been oblivious to everything around him. When he got home that day, he had been bathed in perspiration, which stained his shirt and troubled him. He could not understand any of it.

At the band shell, one of his favorite places in the park, a dozen boys were playing, racing after one another in circles, some game he did not know. He thought of Little Black Sambo, then realized that it was no longer fashionable to remember that sad tale. He saw a boy, possibly fifteen or sixteen, sitting alone on a bench in front of the shell. He pulled the leash, tied it to one of the slats on the bench, and sat down beside the boy. "What brings you here?" he asked the boy.

The boy got up and ran toward the others.

Summer in New York is not exotic. The heat seems to accumulate. Workers move from air-conditioned apartments to air-conditioned offices as expeditiously as possible. Patience frays on subways and buses. For most natives, life goes on, relieved on weekends by hours at public beaches and parks, where hot winds barely soothe.

For teen-age boys the months of June, July and August can be a chance to escape, an invitation to boredom, a taunt to the adventurous. The backward, and some of the very bright, go to summer school. The rich and the docile are packed off to camp. The conscientious may, if lucky, find a part-time summer job as a messenger or a delivery boy at the neighborhood supermarket. The poor settle into the local playground, play basketball tirelessly, walk the streets, guard their coins. Numbed by ennui, some of them get into petty trouble, smoke too much marijuana, pop too many pills.

For some boys the summer is a time for alliances, however transitory, that pass the time. Without a camp to go to or a job to do, they seek out one another early in the summer. For them, summer in New York is a brand-new exploration.

In Manhattan, Central Park is a primary meeting place, and within the park the band shell is a kind of travelers' aid center. In the middle of the park, away from the distractions of the busy areas that surround it, a subculture thrives.

Teen-agers of all persuasions gather to assess one another and to find friendships. Most of all they meet to "hang out." It is, in itself, a pursuit, a kind of purposeful loitering, a lingering in anticipation of something that may never happen, an inactivity that may never develop into activity. It is a sharing of interests, of conversation, of moods and intentions. It can be done while strolling or playing Frisbee or simply sitting on the grass.

At fifteen or sixteen, boys hover between childhood and maturity. They are not sophisticated, yet they wish to seem wise, at least about life on the streets of the city. They cannot for the most part deal with girls as equals; they retreat when challenged by the temptation of sex. They do not plan ahead, as adults might, to get through the summer, the year, their lives. They pause and pass the time. "Hanging out." Despite the urging of parents to "do something," they persist in idling, like a car that is making a sound but is not in motion.

It is an extension of their education, these summer respites, an education that can be acquired only by familiarity with new points of view. It is that that brings them together.

Odd, seemingly incompatible relationships flourish. Ethnic, economic, religious barriers blur or vanish. They have an important mission in common: to get through summer.

Early in this sweltering summer, after the last day of school, three such boys discovered one another at the band shell. They sat on the same bench one day and began to speak. That conversation led to another the next day. They began to meet each morning at the band shell. Gradually they revealed to one another something of their private selves. Whatever their differences, they became a group.

John Samuels, tall, thin and slightly awkward at the age of fifteen, bounded toward the band shell to meet his friends. He felt good. His new Adidas sneakers in glowing shades of bright blue flashed as he ran. He was wearing his Grateful Dead T-shirt and his oldest, most faded paint-splattered jeans. The outfit made him feel relaxed, almost inconspicuous. It was a feeling he liked. Yet he had tenaciously resisted his parents' effort to persuade him to cut his hair; he wore it long, to the middle of his back, in a dangling brown ponytail. It got him some attention, he thought, but not too much of it. He was on the verge of an awareness that he was handsome: a classic American face with luminous green eyes, a ready smile and a slim athletic body.

Any day in the park was an adventure for John. It was new to him. Born and raised in a Long Island suburb, he had moved to Manhattan early this year. After his parents' divorce, his father, who lived in the city, took him to visit the sights every Sunday, and he enjoyed those trips, from the boarding of the new trains in Manhasset to the arrival in Penn Station to his father's good cheer. But it was not the same as living in the city, not as exciting.

When his mother remarried and made the move into the city, John was pleased. He wasn't certain yet how he felt about her new husband; the man was serious and solemn, unlike his own father, who was more tempted by absurdity. But now he could live with his mother and stepfather in Manhattan and visit his father, only a bus ride away. Two homes in the city. The idea delighted him.

But there were other things to deal with. One evening on his way to the large old west side apartment, three nomadic black boys jumped him, seized his tape recorder—a birthday present from his father—and ran off with it. He ran home, five blocks without stop, and told his mother what had happened.

"It isn't easy to live in this city," she said. "It's a frantic place. You can love it one minute and hate it the next. I worry about you. You grew up where there was grass. And trees. And peace. You've got to be careful now. You've got to walk the way good drivers drive. Keep an eye on the others. You know, take care of yourself. In the park too. Remember that."

He paid attention to her. She was the voice of discipline in his life, and if he resented that at times, he knew as well that the rules she set down and the advice she gave were valuable to him. He didn't want to be completely free; he needed her to establish limitations. She was an old friend, he thought.

There were new friends too, boys he had met in the park who were not exactly like those he had known in the suburbs. Not scrubbed, not affluent, not always perceptive and bright. Yet he admired their toughness, their street philosophy, their desire to survive, their wish to create adventure if none existed. They fought boredom daringly. And they spoke a jargon that was new to him, studded with "man" and "baby" and "hip" phrases. He was learning that language, and learning more about the city every day.

Of the many he'd met, he had singled out two to be his friends. It was his first summer in the city, and the two other boys were eager to collaborate—to make it memorable. John went to a private school on the west side; the others attended public schools.

The three of them spent their daytime hours roaming through the park, their evenings in huddles talking about girls they'd never approach, going to films and to rock concerts. Occasionally they would invade the subway yards armed with cans of spray paint and leave their signatures on the sides of subway cars. It had not been John's idea, but when one of his friends suggested it, he felt that despite the risks of arrest and injury it was something he had to do. His mother and father were aware of it; John could not conceal anything from them. They read his face too well. They disapproved and he knew it. He assured them that soon he'd give it up, perhaps when he reached sixteen. He had promised to consider cutting his hair on that birthday as well. There was something odd, he perceived, about having longer hair than his sister, off at college, but it was not a riddle he cared to consider or solve.

On this warm Sunday John was eager to meet Morgan and Markham, his new friends. As he raced along the pavement, he could see them leaning against the front of the band shell. He slapped his palm against theirs, put his arms around them and exhaled. "Whooey, I am feeling good today," he said, and smiled.

Al Morgan was a short, chubby, jovial black who spent most of his days, and some of his nights, in the park. An only child, he lived with his mother and father above a restaurant she owned in Harlem. He attended public school—Julia Richman High School on the east side—coming down to it by bus and subway every day. His father slept during the day and drove a bus at night. Morgan didn't talk with him often. His mother kept busy, in the restaurant or at home, holding off the groping hands of the various men Morgan would discover when he came home late at night.

"Your mother's a whore," one of the neighborhood kids had snapped at him. Morgan wasn't sure, but somehow it didn't matter. He loved her; he could talk to her, which was more than he could say about his relationship with almost anyone else, except perhaps John Samuels and Ronald Markham. She was, he knew, a good woman.

Rose Morgan was in her forties, a small woman, overweight but not fat. When she got dressed up, which she did every evening to look good in her restaurant, Al thought that she was the best-looking woman he'd ever known. Her body was all curves, he had heard a neighbor say admiringly, and Al agreed with the judgment. She wore a great deal of make-up and took great pains to have her hair done regularly. Her lipstick gleamed in the light; not a line on her face seemed to show her age. To Al she seemed to be young, and her perception matched that impression; her words were not the instructional words of a strict mother but the understanding words of a very good friend, and Al enjoyed talking with her. She made good sense, he thought, even when it was hard for him to heed her wishes. When he was away from her, and the temptations of the city streets got to him, he felt guilty about betraying her hopes for him. They would talk about that, easily, and about anything else that either wanted to talk about, except about his father.

"He's a good man and I love him," she said to Al once, "but there's trouble between us that I'll tell you about someday. Not

32

now. Someday." Al hadn't pushed the matter; he was content to have her to talk with.

They would talk for hours. She would tell him about the restaurant, which he'd rarely visit, and how difficult it was to work so hard all day. She would urge him to stay away from writing on subway cars; she didn't want the nuisance of going to the police station to get him and talking to the local precinct's youth officer about her son. She would try to inspire him to work hard at school, to get ready for college. He did work hard, at times, but he found his mind straying in class, and that often meant a word or two from the teacher, a note to his mother, a conference. He couldn't understand what going to college meant, except that it would be harder for him than high school, and he worried about that—when he bothered to think about it at all.

For the most part he met John and Ronald in the park early in the day, and the three of them would explore the park, talk about things that mattered to them and tell one another things they told no one else. Ronald had been caught writing on the wall of the 86th Street Broadway station, but had feigned fear, whined and wept, and the policeman had let him go. He hadn't told his mother. The three boys enjoyed the story. They shared an appreciation of such daring improvisation.

It was comforting to be with his mother and exhilarating to be in the park; Morgan did not like to be alone, anywhere. He structured his life to avoid that, and on days when John and Ronald couldn't be in the park Morgan felt lonely. He did not want to make other new friends; he was satisfied with the two he had. He often called himself "nigger," as other blacks did in jest, and he did not resent it when Samuels and Markham picked up the habit. He knew that they were not bigots.

On this Sunday he was happy to see both of them.

"What'll we do?" he asked the others.

"How about playing some Frisbee?" Ronald asked.

They walked away from the band shell toward the nearby

33

meadow. Ronald had brought the Frisbee. Ronald, in fact, often brought the "equipment." His family had money.

Ronald Markham was not as tall as John Samuels, but he was husky and strong enough at fifteen to be respected for his latent power. "Don't ever get him mad," Samuels had told Morgan. Few provocations did get Markham mad. He rarely flaunted his strength. Only those older guys in the park who chose to challenge him and intimidated him out of his reticence ever discovered the nature of his strength. He fought rarely, and never lost. He had gone to an expensive private school while his parents were still married, but after their divorce his mother moved him into a public high school close to their apartment. He didn't mind. The disorder in the classroom annoyed him, but he managed to study and win respectable, if not outstanding, grades. He had liked the private school but had been offended by the snobbery of some of the students. He found the public school more to his liking, with students who weren't as pretentious and spoiled.

He lived with his mother in an elaborate east side duplex apartment, a co-op she had won in the divorce settlement. His older brother was away at college; his younger sister had her own room in the apartment and rarely came out of it. He was fond of her but really didn't know her very well.

His father had moved to Dallas and remarried. Every six months Ronald and his brother and sister would be sent airline tickets and they'd visit their father and his new wife. It was disconcerting for Ronald. He liked his father, but his father was a bitter man. He said too many bad things about Ronald's mother, and their conversations would escalate to silence rather than screams. The stepmother, as his father insisted on referring to her ("Your stepmother thinks . . ."), seemed ill at ease in Ronald's presence. She was younger than his mother and had never had children of her own.

The visits would last for a few days; the father would give him money and presents, and Ronald would come home to his mother. She would ask questions, would fall into a depression and go off to bed. Too bad that she was out of it so much of the time, Ronald thought, because she was a beautiful woman: tall, thin, with long brown hair and pale blue eyes. She could have been a fashion model, Ronald believed, if she had had the energy to do it. He didn't understand what went on in her head.

She led a curious life, and Ronald knew it. She took all sorts of pills. Some made her very calm. Ronald assumed those were Valium; he had taken one once, getting it for a dollar from a dealer in the park, and had felt weary more than anything else. Other pills perked her up. She would take one of those late at night and would then, after midnight, be picked up by a man in a limousine. She always came home before Ronald woke up, and she was in place in her bed on a stack of pillows drinking orange juice and coffee by the time Ronald got up for school or, now, to go to the park to meet his friends. Whatever she did with that man, it did not seem to make her feel better or worse. She simply *did* it. Ronald wondered if they had a late meal somewhere at some luxurious midtown restaurant, and he wondered if such restaurants were open that late. He wondered if they went to the man's apartment and talked and drank expensive wine or champagne and fucked. It baffled Ronald, but he rarely talked to his mother about such things.

He felt self-sufficient most of the time, and rather than listen to his mother's hypochondriacal muttering he solved his own problems rather than bring them to her. He felt sorry for her when she raved on about the danger of cancer. She talked about that whenever she was on an anti-smoking kick. Much of the time, however, she talked about her own pains and ailments, and that usually made Ronald want to get out of the apartment. After all, he had concluded, she had a doctor to tell all that to.

For Markham, like Samuels and Morgan, the park was the place to be, especially on a day like this when the sun was warm but not too hot, the sky was a perfect blue and his friends were available and in good spirits.

The threesome cut through the crowd. They were all in jeans, all in T-shirts. Samuels and Morgan wore sneakers; Markham wore Western boots. As they walked, Morgan's tightly cropped Afro bobbed between the two ponytails. They wriggled through the horde of people that had collected at the band shell. A resident pusher waved and asked Morgan if they wanted to buy anything. Morgan didn't pause; he simply shook his head. The three passed by a uniformed cop from the Central Park precinct, his hands on his belt, almost dozing on his feet, staring vacantly at the crowd. Three young girls in platform shoes, short skirts and tight-fitting blouses walked toward the three boys.

"Hmmmmmm," Morgan hummed.

"Uh-huh," John agreed.

"Slurp," Ronald added.

The girls walked on, and the three boys made their way toward the field of grass. Morgan broke ahead and Ronald tossed the Frisbee at him. It sailed over his head.

For a few minutes they tossed the plastic disc back and forth adeptly. Then, bored, they sat down on the grass and stared up at the sky.

"What's happenin'?" Morgan said.

"Not much. I think I'm having dinner with my father. You know what that means? It means steak and mashed potatoes. He isn't much of a cook," John offered.

"But he's a good dude, right?" Morgan said.

"Definitely."

Ronald rolled over on his stomach and looked at the mall, clogged with Sunday gawkers. He saw that older man with his furry dog, the man who had sat down beside him while he waited for Morgan and John to arrive. He wondered briefly if the man was a fag, a word the three applied to almost any man they didn't like. This man was moving along briskly, clutching the leash as the dog strained to move forward. Ronald rolled over again.

36

"How about a movie?" John asked.

"I don't have any bread," Morgan said.

"I've got enough for all of us," Ronald volunteered.

"Beautiful," Morgan said.

"Quite," John said. The three laughed at his parody of a film Englishman.

"Let's do that later," Morgan suggested.

"What about now?" Ronald asked.

"Let's hustle our asses down to the fountain," Morgan said, pointing toward the Bethesda Fountain, "and see some freaks."

"Another Sunday in the park," John said.

"Right," Morgan agreed.

The three boys rose and bounded toward the fountain.

Warren Jackson touched Mary's upper arm and traced a path toward her shoulder. Mary Hodges, you are a good-looking woman, he thought, a good-looking woman. But what is there about her that troubles me? he asked himself. They were walking through Central Park. The sky was flawlessly blue and the sun was warm, but not too hot yet.

"What are you thinking?" Mary asked.

"Nothing," Jackson answered.

"There is no such thing as thinking nothing," she said.

"Were my lips moving?" he said.

"Never mind."

He scanned her willowy body, her beige skin, her compact Afro, her shining lipstick; he surveyed it all. They had met at a party a month ago; he had seen her through the crowd and had gotten to her.

"What do you do?" she had asked him.

"I'm a cop," he had told her.

"No shit," she had screeched.

"Don't worry," he had assured her, "I'm not here to seize that joint you're smoking."

They had gone back to his place that night and had been seeing each other once or twice a week ever since. Much of it was fine, he thought, but something was missing. He did not know what, but whatever it was, he missed it.

"What's been happening?" she asked, interrupting his introspection.

"Where?"

"On your job."

"I've been in Queens all week," he said. "We were trying to land a pusher, and most of the time I spent leaning against a wall looking like a drunk."

"Did he show up?"

"Eventually."

"And?"

"And I got to him first, made a buy and told him his good luck had ended."

"What did he do?"

"He offered me three thousand dollars to let him split before my friends joined us."

"Was he black?"

"Yes. Like me. Like you. But different."

"Does that bother you?"

"Which? The three thousand or the fact that he was black?"

"Both."

"Well, I looked at the money and I wanted it. For some clothes or a car or some of the things I don't have. But I didn't take it. I don't take it. Understand?"

"No, good boy, I don't. You earn peanuts on that job. Who would know?"

"I would know."

"You are a black Jesus."

"Bullshit."

"Okay. Did it bother you to nail another black? Don't the blacks have enough trouble? Don't we?"

"We have trouble, Mary. We have it. And I know it. You don't want to hear my speech about the law and how I do my job. Not now."

"I don't dig morality lessons, Warren, from anyone."

They walked through the park in silence. What she doesn't know about me, Jackson thought, is the story of my life. He had not told her much. Some of it skittered through his head as they strolled.

His father had been a famous jazz musician, a tenor saxophone player, Jay Jay Jackson, who drank too much. His mother kept whatever money she could out of what he earned, put it away out of sight. It never amounted to much, but they weren't poor. His father made records, which were reviewed reverentially; women called often, asking for him. But he wasn't home very often. He traveled and played and his fans remained loyal to him. He drank, and concert promoters who wanted to be sure he went on stage poured more liquor into him.

He died of it all, the drink and the deprivation and the bad meals in obscure towns, but every time he spent a few hours with his son, his only child, there was love between them. Jackson remembered that. His father had not been evil, only self-destructive, and out of his example Jackson had found some guidance for himself. Be able to love and stay out of trouble.

Jay Jay died when Jackson was in high school, and he felt the loss. His mother worked, as a social worker, but there wasn't much surplus cash around the house. After high school he entered CCNY, a public college, and his mother gave him money for clothes and books and something extra for the girls on weekends. By the time he was graduated in 1968 he knew he could not be a stereotype, a funky nigger. A few months later he joined the police force. Later he wondered what he would do if he had to bust one of his father's friends, one of the musicians he knew who were hung up on heroin. It hadn't come up yet.

He made progress in the force. His life was ordered. He had his own neat apartment. He had money to spend and was not depressed by the idea that he would never be rich. He felt supe-

39

rior to the wealthy pimps he had arrested. He would not be a caricature of a black; he was not ashamed of his blackness, but he wanted to be himself. Whenever he added "man" to the end of a sentence, he felt like a phony. He didn't do *that*, even with women who did it to him, expecting him to respond in kind. Women did find him appealing. He was tall enough, at six feet, and bright enough to attract smart women. He was not the prototype of the black stud, but the mythology preceded him and he found it necessary at times to explain to women that he was Warren Jackson, not Jim Brown. Privately he knew that he had grown his beard because he felt it enhanced his resemblance to Walt Frazier, the basketball player; he was pleased when the similarity was acknowledged. Mary had not yet mentioned it; she knew little about sports.

"Remember that night when we met?" Mary asked.

"Sure."

"And I laughed because you were a cop."

"Yes."

"I still feel strange about it."

"Why?"

"Where I lived, they weren't on our side."

"Too bad."

"Yes. Baby, we were poor, and everything we did that was the slightest bit off center got the attention of those wonderful men in blue."

She had been poor. Jackson remembered the conversation in which she had told him. They were at a fancy east side restaurant and she had put her fork down, had looked at him and said, "What the hell am I doing here?" She answered her own question: "Because I belong here." And she did. While her family had disintegrated around her in Harlem—her father vanishing, her mother working at menial jobs, her sister married at fifteen and gone—she studied, did well in high school and won a scholarship to Smith. She did very well in those four years and went from Smith to a job on the creative side of an advertising agency. Now,

40

two jobs later, she was earning $25,000 a year, supervised a staff of artists and copywriters and was an independent woman at the age of twenty-six. She chose her men with care, because there were many to choose from, and Jackson had been her current choice, ever since that night at the party.

Together they formed an attractive couple. Jackson dressed well on his limited budget and Mary dressed well on her larger budget. "We're looking good," she would say as they went out.

They were at the Conservatory Water, on the east side of the park near 74th Street. They watched the children manipulate their model boats in mock skirmishes and elegant cruises. They studied the weekend tennis players, sweating on their way to and from the crowded courts on the west side.

"Let's keep moving," Jackson said. "I am in perpetual danger."

"You are super safe with me," she said.

They walked to the mall, between rows of American elms, and surveyed the vendors, mimes, jugglers, street theater, steel drum bands, guitarists, Frisbee enthusiasts and assorted freaks. They walked along the Pergola, behind the band shell.

"You took the job because you wanted power," Mary said.

"Maybe. You took *your* job because you wanted power," he replied.

"Right. But I've got power *and* money and you've just got power."

"Ah, so it comes out into the open," he said, feeling challenged. "Well, listen to me. Pay attention. I don't use that power to make money. I don't care about that. I make enough to do what I want to do. And I don't go around pushing people around, letting them know that Warren Jackson has got power. Understand me. I chose this job because it seemed to me that it had to be done and done properly. I mean *done*. And not just by dumb guys who had been doing it for so long that they'd forgotten how to do it. I didn't sleep through school and I don't sleep on the job now. I work, and the better I can do it the better I feel. A lot of it is pure boring shit. Paperwork. Forms. But when it works for me, and it does, it is like solving a puzzle. Some people are crossword-puzzle nuts and some people are doctors and some are scientists, and that's all just fine with me. I'm a cop and that's fine with me too."

"You believe that you are being helpful to others? Is that it?"

"Sort of. Yes. And I resent it when people ridicule that."

"Do you ever think that one day you'll get killed? Shot by some idiot who doesn't know you?"

"Never."

"Let's continue this at some later date," she said, scowling.

"Let's."

They walked down to the band shell, and as they got there Jackson spotted a group of older boys menacing a younger one. He saw a knife flash in the sunlight and he broke away from Mary and moved toward the group. He rarely got involved in his off-duty hours, but this, he concluded spontaneously, would be an exception.

He ran up to the boy with the knife and wrenched it out of his hand, folded its blade out of sight and put the knife into his pocket. The other boys stepped back.

"I'm ready if you're ready," he shouted.

Three of the older boys glared at him, then they peeled off and walked away.

"Get out," he shouted at the one who had held the knife. That one moved along lazily, arrogantly.

Jackson turned to the boy who had been threatened. Mary walked up beside him.

"What was that all about?" Jackson asked.

"Who knows?" the boy said. "Craziness. They picked me out, for a donation. They figured I wouldn't fight back; all they wanted was money. Payment to go away."

"Why didn't you give it to him?"

"I don't have any. But he wouldn't believe me."

"And if you had some?"

42

"I don't know if I'd have given it to him or not."

"Jackson's my name. What's yours?"

"Samuels. John Samuels."

"It's a nice day, John. Not a time for trouble."

"You know," Samuels said, "you look like Walt Frazier."

Jackson smiled. "I'm not tall enough and I'm not that kind of star."

Jackson never had brothers or sisters, and kids of all sizes and ages interested him. He wondered what they thought about, how they got into trouble or avoided it, what it was like to be a kid in Manhattan these days.

"You live around here?" Jackson asked.

"Not far."

"Is this where you spend your time?"

"When there's no school, I hang out here. Don't do too much."

"You don't get bored?"

"No. There's stuff to do."

"What?"

"Frisbee. A little ball. Movies. Moving around the city. My parents wanted me to go to camp. Never."

"Why?"

"It sucks. You know, organized games and that sort of shit. Now we row our boats, now we make pottery, now we eat and now we sleep."

There was something about the boy, about his easy manner, that Jackson liked.

"What do you do?" Samuels asked.

"I work."

"Of course you work. What kind of work?"

"The worst kind, and the best."

"You don't want to talk about it."

"Not now."

"Okay."

"Well . . ." Jackson began.

"You talk funny," Samuels said.

"What do you mean I talk funny?"

"I don't know. You just do. The words you use. The way you fit them together."

"You mean, my buddy John, that I am black and I don't talk like I'm black."

"Maybe. But don't get unhappy about it."

"I am who I am, that's all. Dig it, baby? I mean, man, what's happenin'?"

Samuels giggled.

Jackson put out his hand and Samuels shook it, then ran off toward a group of boys his own age at the edge of the band shell.

Mary put her hand in Jackson's and pulled him toward the walk north. "Good kid," she said. "Ever wonder what kind of a father you'd make?"

"Never," Jackson said.

They continued their walk, past a shack with graffiti all over it: WIZARD, SCOOTCH 101, SCALE, THE DEMON. As they walked, Jackson recognized a few familiar faces, minor-league pushers peddling LSD and marijuana and sleeping pills, but he decided to abstain. He led Mary to the lake beneath the Belvedere Castle. When they got there they sat down, watched the birds, watched the children play, in silence.

She broke the silence. "When that pusher offered you the money, did you tell any of the other cops on the case?"

"Yes. I mentioned it."

"What did they say?"

"One of them wondered why I didn't take it. I told him."

"Was he black or white?"

"White."

"Did it bother you?"

"Yes," he said. "Let's go back to your place."

They got up and went to Mary's apartment on Central Park West.

An hour later her phone rang, for Jackson. His commanding officer always knew where to find him. The park precinct needed

help on a case, a homicide. The request had gone through chan-
nels and Jackson had been assigned to it, at the Precinct Captain's
request.

Fine, Jackson thought, I spent the day doing research.

Monday

"I can't seem to fall asleep at night. And when I do, finally, I have a terrible time getting up in the morning," Wilton said.

"Is this new, recent?"

"I think so. I can't remember having that particular problem before."

"Is something bothering you? Are you obsessing about something?"

"I don't think so."

"Well, try going to an Antonioni film, *any* Antonioni film."

"Don't be frivolous."

"I'm not. Every time I go to one, I doze off."

"I don't go to films often."

"Yes, I remember."

Dr. Weinstein, round and middle-aged, squirmed in his large leather chair, his head cocked slightly to see the framed degrees on his office wall.

"What should I do?"

"Do you want me to prescribe something?"

"Not really. I just want to know what is happening to me."

"Maybe nothing is happening. I mean nothing serious. Maybe you're simply bored."

"Bored? That's possible, I suppose. I do lead an ordered life.

49

But I've always thought I liked it that way."

"Well. Do you?"

"Why do you ask? After all these months, don't you know me as well as I know myself?"

"Not exactly."

"I live in that marvelous apartment. I once invited you to visit."

"Yes, but I didn't accept."

"Why?"

"I'd rather not. I don't like to invade the lives of my patients in that way."

"At any rate, it is a lovely apartment, everything in its place, everything of quality. I see it at times as my personal museum. I have one wall filled with model soldiers. You know about that?"

"Yes, an expensive hobby."

"I can afford it. And the paintings. The very good ones I keep for myself. I sell the trash to others. Yesterday a gross woman from White Plains came in and asked to see the work of that man who does those 'squiggles.' It took almost an hour to find out what she meant. Miró. I sold her a dreadful piece. She left absolutely delighted, in ecstasy. God, she was repulsive. So grotesquely fat. Fat."

"Uh-huh."

"By the way, you are getting obese yourself."

"Please, don't go into that."

"You are."

"Don't be hostile."

"I'm not. I'm being factual."

"Perhaps. But you're still being hostile."

"Can't I speak to you that way?"

"It's still hostile."

"Why have I been coming here for all these months?"

"Do you have to ask?"

"Yes, or I wouldn't ask, would I?"

"You tell me."

"Because I haven't had many close friends, and I think of you more as a friend than my doctor. And when my mother died almost a year ago, I had to talk to someone I could trust."

"Okay."

"Common enough, I suppose, and very expensive."

"Do you think of it as money, as a wasted investment?"

"No, actually, I don't. I've needed it."

"Then tell me about your problem sleeping."

"I don't know. I spend a day at the gallery. I do well at it. I put the money into my swelling savings account. I go home. I arrange the soldiers. I read. I put on my pajamas and get into bed. I stare. My eyes won't shut."

"Why?"

"Honestly, I don't know. I'm not a fool. You know that. I am a rational man. I do what I do and I know *why*. In this case, I simply don't understand it. When I was a child my mother would come in and wake me up, gently and lovingly. I still remember that. Vividly. She would have breakfast ready and I would enjoy getting up. Now I don't want to get up, and it isn't just because I haven't gotten enough sleep."

"Are you tired of running the gallery?"

"Not really. It can be depressing, of course. There are horrifying days. But, generally, no. I'm surrounded by what I love, by beauty. That may sound pompous or pretentious and I don't mean it to sound that way. I go to Europe every year and I see people I've dealt with for years and we get along very well. At home it's different. I don't have very many friends. I don't exactly know why. I'm too judgmental perhaps. Most people offend me, their manners, their values, their deceptions, their betrayals. It is not, you understand, that I must have a large group of admirers fawning over me. Or that I miss all those parties that everyone else seems to attend. I don't. I'd rather be at home, in comfort, than standing around aimlessly holding a drink I don't want to drink, pretending to be friendly when I don't feel friendly."

"I see. Then what is it?"

"I'm fifty-five years old. I shouldn't have this sort of problem. My life should be tranquil."

"Much of it is tranquil, isn't it?"

"Yes, but apparently not enough of it. Or something is missing."

"You do have Bernard, right?"

"Certainly and he is a handsome, affectionate animal. I suppose I chose him because he was. I had heard that chows could be vicious, resentful, vengeful, but he isn't any of those. Sometimes at night, after a horrendous day at the gallery, we sit together on the sofa side by side. His thick, wonderful red fur. At times I think he is smiling at me. Don't say anything. I know how pet owners delude themselves."

"He is a friend?"

"Of sorts. I'm not crazy."

"You'd prefer another sort of friend, one who speaks?"

"Maybe."

"A woman? Have you met any lately?"

"Not really. A striking woman came into the gallery. Tall, slim, long blond hair, in her forties. I thought about her days after I'd met her. But I couldn't recall her name and don't know what I would have done even if I had. I haven't been with a woman in years."

"I know."

"Yes, you do."

"A man?"

"No. Somehow men bore me. I cannot bear their company for very long. You are an exception. I needn't tell you that."

"Thank you."

"Never mind."

"Are you afraid of anything?"

"Of getting old, I mean truly old, yes. I try to take care of myself. I buy the best clothes. I try to eat sensibly and to stay in good condition. I weigh today what I did twenty years ago. My teeth are mine. My internist tells me that I am in excellent health. Nevertheless I am reminded of the inevitable. I want to live as long as I can. I don't want to think of life as an allowance."

"Must you?"

"Yes, I must. I want the best. I look around the room every day when I lunch at Les Pleiades. Do you know the place? On East Seventy-sixth. Fine restaurant. The place is filled with young men and women, both with long hair, giggling, smiling, touching each other. When I look at them, and I'm usually alone at lunch, I envy them and hate them simultaneously."

"Why?"

"They will be there, at those tables, eating that sole, when I am gone."

"Indeed. That troubles you?"

"Of course it does."

"Why?"

"Perhaps because I know that I could be gone tomorrow and no one would notice."

"That's not so. I would care."

"You, yes. Who else?"

"You tell me."

"No one."

"Really?"

"Really."

"Why?"

"I don't know. I do know that there are lunatics in this city who kill without reason, who kill for a dime or a purse or for nothing. I don't want to be such a victim."

"Why do you think you will be?"

"I don't. But I think about it. There are valuable works in my gallery. If they want to break in at night, fine, let them. I'm insured. But what if they come in during the day, when I'm alone? What do I do then?"

"I don't know. What?"

"I bought a gun. Did I tell you that?"

"No."

"It is tiny, almost a replica of one of those old pirate pistols. I liked the way it looked, first. Then I realized that I ought to have one around, just in case. I don't know if I could use it, but I wanted to have it. You can hold it in your palm and no one would know. I bought some ammunition for it, a few bullets, not an arsenal's worth."

"And you would use it?"

"It is funny. Yes, I might use it, to defend myself. But you know how much I hate noise."

"Yes."

"The sound of a gun going off would offend me as much as the use of the gun itself. I mentioned it to the super at the gallery building. He laughed. Easy to make a silencer, he told me. I laughed. I paid him twenty-five dollars and he made one. I don't understand how he did it, but he did it, in two days. So now I have it, gun and silencer, in a drawer in my desk at the gallery. It all strikes me as odd, as if I were a spectator of my own behavior, laughing at myself for succumbing to that sort of fear."

"Perhaps it's that fear that keeps you awake at night?"

"Perhaps. But I am safe at home. I don't sit there afraid of intruders. My building is a fort, impossible to penetrate. The night doorman, I suspect, is in training for the Mafia. He is not gracious. The perfect doorman. So why should I worry at night? I don't."

"Think about it and we'll talk about it again at our next session."

"Is this one over?"

"Almost."

"I see."

"Just a few minutes left. Anything else you want to talk about today?"

"I am trying to be less anti-social. Not easy at my age. When I walk Bernard in Central Park there are moments when I want to find someone to talk with. Sometimes I try to talk to the boys

54

in Central Park. There was one a few days ago, but I can't remember much about him. I think he was one of those idiots the public school system is cranking out these days. Nothing on his mind. He didn't know what I was talking about. I got up and left."

"Time's up," Dr. Weinstein said, rising out of his chair and moving around the desk. He put his arm around Edmund Wilton's shoulder and led him to the door. "See you in a few days," he said.

"Of course," Wilton answered.

The next patient was in the small waiting room—a tiny intense woman who avoided his gaze; she peered at her opened copy of *Cosmopolitan.* As he walked out, Wilton thought, How could the doctor talk to people like that? What did they have to say to interest him?

He opened the door and went out into the summer sun, back to the gallery.

My God, the doctor thought, he is a dull man, as he greeted his next patient. And she's not exactly a winner, he thought, as he guided her into his office, touching her shoulder and smiling.

John Samuels, Al Morgan and Ronald Markham sat on the steps of the Museum of Natural History and smoked. They watched the customary procession of morning sun seekers into the park, making their way on foot, jogging, on bikes, pushing babies in strollers, carrying picnic baskets, stoned, giddy, lazy, all segments of the city's escapist population. The boys watched them without comment.

"Man, how *do* you smoke this shit?" Morgan grunted, smiling at Samuels. He had, as usual, borrowed a cigarette from Samuels, who carried them; Morgan's mother forbade him to carry them.

"That, my friend, is an authentic Lark," Samuels said. "It will keep you free of cancer."

"It will keep me free of smoke, baby. Drawin' on that is like trying' to get a breeze out of a flat tire."

"It's free, man."

"Beautiful," Morgan said. "Beautiful."

Markham didn't speak. He was the quiet one, strong, self-sufficient and silent.

"Want one?" Samuels asked him.

"No. I don't smoke and you know it."

"You smoke and I know it, but you don't smoke these," Samuels said.

"Right. If I'm gonna get cancer, I'm gonna get stoned first."

"What do we do today?" Morgan asked.

"I want to buy a knife," Samuels said.

"Why?" Markham asked.

"For self-protection. After that scene yesterday, I want to have something on my side. I'm tired of giving up my bread to some cat poking a knife at me."

"You wouldn't use it, baby. You know you wouldn't," Morgan said.

"Probably true. But I want to have one." His father had given him ten dollars.

They walked to the subway and took a B train to 42nd Street. Emerging, the three boys peered around; they did not often get to that part of the city.

"I heard about this store that sells souvenirs and knives," Samuels said, looking west along 42nd Street past the row of cheap movie theaters, fast food restaurants and decaying buildings. The three boys walked along, heading toward Eighth Avenue, trying to look inconspicuous. A few drunks slept against buildings. Pairs of junkies floated past. A pimp was having an argument with one of his prostitutes. Samuels found the store and moved into the entryway to peer at the knives in the window; Morgan and Markham joined him.

"There's one for four ninety-five," Samuels said, pointing to a black and silver switchblade. "And there's one for twelve bucks," a hunting knife."

"Man, let's split," Morgan said. "I don't dig this neighborhood."

"Soon," Samuels said, "soon."

It was Morgan who realized that they were not alone.

"Mmmm," he hummed, to get Samuels' attention. The three turned toward the street and saw three tall black teen-agers, edging toward them.

"No trouble," one of the blacks said. "No trouble." He had a knife in his hand, the blade barely visible. "Just lay your watch on us. We dig it," he said, pointing to Samuels' wristwatch, a recent gift from his father.

"Here's the watch," Samuels said, slipping it off his wrist and pointing it at the blacks. At that moment, a customer emerged from the store. Samuels heard the door open. In an instant, he yelled, "Go, go, go," and broke through the cordon, along with Morgan and Markham.

Markham raced east on 42nd Street, ran through traffic and disappeared down Broadway. Morgan ran across 42nd and headed west. Samuels dashed toward Eighth Avenue, the three blacks after him.

He ran as fast as he could and could not shake the blacks, who remained a few feet behind him. Along the way, people watched, and did nothing about it. At Eighth Avenue, Samuels spotted a trash basket at the corner, with an empty gin bottle in it. He paused in his run, reached into the basket and grabbed the bottle. He turned. The three pursuers were almost up to him; he smashed the bottle at their feet, and when they stopped he ran into the nearby subway station. A train was ready to pull out; he got into it just as the doors were closing.

He did not know where Morgan and Markham had gone, but they must have survived, he thought as he headed uptown on the train. He felt the pounding of his heart and wiped the sweat off his face. He realized that he was still clutching his watch; he had not given it up. He felt good about that. He got off the train uptown and headed for his favorite rendezvous point in the park, the band shell. If the others didn't run into any trouble, they'd be there too, in time.

Within an hour, Morgan and Markham arrived.

"Man, forget what I said about not buying a knife. You should get yourself one," Morgan suggested.

"One of these days I will," Samuels said.

"Let's just rest," Markham said, still breathing heavily from the memory of his midtown run.

They sat in front of the band shell. Two teen-agers, one male and one female but looking identical with long blond hair, leaned against a nearby tree and passed a cigarette back and forth; when they smiled at each other, both revealed the gleam of braces. A middle-aged man with long flowing gray hair and a stained velvet jump suit in a floral print glided gracefully through the park holding his sunglasses up in the air as an offering to an undefined god. A tall, husky black slightly older than the three boys strolled up to them.

"Phillips," Samuels called.

"Hey, baby," Phillips said. "Good to see your ugly face."

"You are one dumb cat," Samuels said.

"Watch who you call what," Phillips said.

"Do not injure that white man," Morgan said.

"I will bust his ass if I wish," Phillips said.

"What's happenin'?" Morgan asked.

"Not much, baby. I ain't got no bread. I ain't got no chick. I'm just hangin' out," Phillips volunteered.

"Hell yes you are," Morgan said. "What you sellin'?"

"I ain't sellin' shit today, man."

"Some good grass for the city folk, for the underprivileged?"

"Nothin'. I mean nothin'." Phillips waved his arms in the air and walked away aimlessly.

"I was just lookin' for a little charity," Morgan said, "and he had nothin' to give."

"Charity from him?" Samuels asked.

"Do not say that. My black brother back there has the dignity of his race. Dig?"

"And they'll bust him for dealing, right here, one of these days," Samuels said.

"And then, my man, he will be another dumb nigger," Morgan said, smiling.

"Gentlemen."

Samuels turned to see who had spoken. It was a uniformed policeman. Morgan and Markham turned too.

"Uh-huh," Samuels said.

"I have a problem," the policeman said.

"You sure do, man," Morgan said.

"And I want to talk to you about it."

"Sure," Samuels said.

"Any of you know a kid named Torres? Chico Torres?"

"A Rican?" Markham asked.

"Yeah."

"Why?" Samuels asked.

"Do you know him? Your age. Your size. May like to hang out in the park. Know him?"

"Don't know the name, man," Morgan said. "Where's he from?"

"Up in East Harlem, lives with his mother up there. Or did."

"I don't know him," Samuels said.

"Me neither," Markham added.

"No," Morgan said. "Don't believe I do."

"Why?" Samuels asked.

"Do you read the papers?"

"No." "No." "No."

"This kid, Torres, is dead. Near here. We found his body, with one hole in it, in the heart. One bullet, one shot, one dead Rican."

"Jesus," Samuels said.

"We don't know who or why, and we better know both soon or we're in trouble."

"Jesus," Samuels said again.

"If any of you hear anything or see anything you think might help us out, you let me know, right? Name's Goldman. Central Park precinct."

"Right," Samuels said.

The boys watched as Goldman moved on toward the edge of the band shell, where he spoke to several Puerto Rican teenagers, including several who had been singing and dancing on the stage itself.

Markham's mother was home when he got in and, as she often was, was in bed watching television. His father sent her money regularly and she spent most of it making herself comfortable. Markham walked into her bedroom and waved.

"Where were you today?" she asked.

"In the park," he answered. He decided to tell her about the adventure in Times Square, as well.

After he did, she screamed at him. "Why, why, why? Why do you get involved in things like that? Why do you go to that part of the city? You must not do that."

He decided not to tell her about Chico Torres, whoever he was. He assured her that he would stay away from Times Square, and then he went to his room to read the latest issue of *Playboy*. The magazine was beginning to appeal to him.

Morgan got home during one of his mother's breaks from working in the restaurant she owned downstairs. She was sipping a cup of coffee when he entered. She put down the cup and tapped him lovingly on the shoulder. "Good to see you, Al," she said. "Very good to see you."

"Nice to see you, too, Momma," he said.

He thought about telling her the story of the trouble in Times Square, but it would have meant telling her about the three black boys, and she wouldn't have liked that part at all. And she didn't know Samuels or Markham, so not much of that story would have really mattered to her. And he didn't want to mention Torres, because he didn't want to think about that. His mother would get upset about that news, he thought; she had seen kids killed on the street and she got all worked up whenever she recited the stories for Al's benefit.

He kissed her on the cheek and went to his room, where he relaxed on his bed. He heard the door open and shut and knew that she had gone back to the restaurant. It felt good to be alone in his room.

Samuels visited his father on the east side and told him about both the Times Square escape and the death of Torres.

"Damnedest city in the world to live in," his father said. "If I were you, I wouldn't buy a knife. You might just use it and add to all the other nutsy things that go on here. Hard to say what the Torres thing means. It happens too often in New York."

Samuels drank a Coke and got up to go. "I saved the watch," he said, pointing to his wrist.

"Good," his father said. "Good move."

Samuels took the crosstown bus to the west side and got home as his mother and her husband were going to bed.

"Do much today?" she asked.

"No," he answered.

"Get some rest," she said.

He went into his room and closed the door, put on a Led Zeppelin record and stretched out on his bed. He thought about Torres and wondered why he was worried about someone he had never known. Then he realized that he was worried about himself, as well. He'd have to be careful, he thought, if that was possible.

Tuesday

Jackson got up at seven-thirty. He could hear Mary in the shower, getting ready for her job at the ad agency. He went into the kitchen and poured a cup of coffee and thought about her.

He hadn't been drawn so close to a woman since his junior year at CCNY in 1967, when he had gotten involved with another man's wife. Their meetings were held in secret; she said it was love. He decided then to stay away from married women and to stay away as well from anything too intimate, from anything too involving. Until Mary, that had worked. He didn't know what to do about that. So he thought about Torres.

Yesterday he had reported to the park precinct, had talked to the Captain, to Fahey and to Goldman, whom he hadn't seen since their days at the police academy.

"Torres. A clean kid. Respectable mother, father out of it," Goldman had told him. "The kid comes to the park, alone apparently, and when we find him, sort of resting on the grass, there's a bullet hole in him. One neat hole, close range. So close, in fact, that there may not have been any air between the barrel and the kid's chest. Like that."

"What do you think?" Jackson had asked Goldman.

"I don't know what to think about it. Did the kid have an enemy? How the hell do I know? We can't find one. I know that much. And if he did have an enemy, why did the guy want him dead? What could the kid have done to deserve that? And if he wanted to kill the kid, why do it in the park? Why not somewhere else, hide the body or dump it? We've got hundreds of questions. No answers."

"Caliber?"

"Twenty-two. We know that, or at least Ballistics knows that. Not much else."

"You talked to the kid's mother?"

"Three of us did. Nothing. Absolutely nothing. A nice woman, hysterical, confused, troubled. All of his friends were good boys, she said."

"So you're looking for a lunatic?" Jackson had asked.

"Wonderful. A lunatic. You know how many lunatics we've got in the park? You know how many lunatics we've got in the city who spend part of their lives in the park? You know how many lunatics there are right now playing ball out there in the meadow? The Captain is leaning on Fahey; and Fahey, the good sergeant, is leaning on us. Meaning you too. Be alert, he says. Be wise cops. We're lucky in one respect. The story appeared in the papers, but it didn't get much space. Just another homicide. A kid named Torres, that's all."

Jackson had left Goldman and had walked through the park for hours.

He found nothing to contribute to his understanding of the case. Today he would do more of the same.

Mary came into the kitchen, fully dressed and fragrant.

"You are a walking rose," he said. "Why don't you get to work late today?"

"Save it for some other time," she said, smiling.

"Do I get interest if I save it?" he asked.

"You've got that already, love," she said. She had not used that word with him before, and she seemed embarrassed. He got up and kissed her gently on the forehead. She left and he got dressed and headed for the precinct.

Goldman was out on patrol, so he talked to the Captain for a few minutes, then chatted wth Fahey. No new leads. Fahey seemed increasingly frustrated; it had, Jackson thought, something to do with having a teen-age kid, and something to do with being a proud cop.

Jackson walked into the park and roamed. It was another hot day, but it didn't bother him. It was better than sitting against a wall in Queens and waiting.

Wednesday

It was Wilton's regular eight A.M. session.

"You look awful," the doctor said.

"I *feel* awful."

"Why?"

"I don't know exactly. I'm supposed to be in good health for my age. I don't have a heart condition or arthritis or high blood pressure or hardening of the arteries."

"Well?"

"I'm fifty-five years old, and when I'm alone I think about how much time I've wasted and how much time I have left and I fall into a depression."

"Why don't you close the gallery during the summer, like most of the others do?"

"I don't because I don't want to go off to some idiotic summer place and watch all those idiots cavort. I like the gallery during the summer. It's quiet, certainly, but I like that. I like the city in summertime."

The doctor swiveled slowly in his chair from side to side. He made a soft sucking sound.

"Don't do that. It distracts me."

"Don't do what?"

"Don't make that noise, that sucking noise."

"Oh. Something caught in my teeth. A piece of toast, a fragment."

"I see. Don't do it, please."

"All right."

"I like walking through the park. I always have. And I do it almost every day. Then at night I can't go to sleep. I turn on the radio or try to read a book or get up and have some sort of snack. When I'm lucky I fall asleep at three or four in the morning, then I don't want to get up at eight or nine. I think I mentioned that during our last session."

"Yes, you did."

"I take Bernard for walks in the park whenever I feel like it. I lock the gallery and go home and get him and we walk through the park. I sit in the zoo and watch the children and their mothers. The children love that place, and when I hear them giggle and see them running around happily I feel better. I laugh at the seals too, and the monkeys. My God, monkeys are odd and wonderful. I stare at the lions and tigers and admire their grace and wonder how they manage to keep their sanity in those cages. I want to free them."

"You do?"

"Yes. But I wouldn't, of course, even if I knew how. Whenever the thought occurs to me, I just tug at Bernard and we walk north, past the zoo."

"Where?"

"Nowhere in particular. I look at the flowers. Does it ever seem to you that the park is filled with lovely flowers?"

"Not really. I don't walk there often."

"Chrysanthemum, sassafras, flowering dogwood, elderberry, lily of the valley. They're all there."

"I didn't know that. I'm not sure I'd know one if I saw one."

"I know them all. I see people pulling at them, stepping on them, and I want to have them arrested. When I start to feel that way, I go home. There's nothing I can do about it. I heard that there is a club that tries to protect the trees and flowers in the park, but I've never wanted to join it."

"Yes."

"How did I get onto *that?*"

"You were talking about how you feel."

"Of course. It has something to do with the rituals of my life, I think. Everything so ordered. My apartment, my gallery, my dog. I want to alter it, but I'm afraid to alter it."

"Do you try?"

"Rarely. I went to a cocktail party a few weeks ago. I sat in a corner and watched the others. A young bearded painter whose name I've forgotten, impersonating an adolescent Matisse. His work is dreadful, but he sells it. I can't even talk to him. He disgusts me. Two gay women who collaborate on large canvases the size of entire walls. Can you believe that? Two signatures, one cluttered style. A pretentious competitor of mine who runs one of those chic galleries on Fifty-seventh Street. We've known each other for years, but we've rarely spoken to each other in more than monosyllables. I can't bear those parties. I had one drink and left."

The doctor looked at his watch.

"Is it time for me to leave?"

"No, not really. We have time."

"Then why did you look at your watch?"

"To find out how much time we did have."

"Is that how your life is ordered? By time?"

"Not really. But I do have that responsibility. I do have to know where I am, in the progression."

"So you won't give one patient a bargain, an extra few minutes, and short-change another?"

"I don't worry about that. It doesn't happen."

"Then don't worry about it now, with me."

"Of course. Sorry."

"Thank you."

"What else do you feel these days?"

"Empty."

"I gather. But how?"

"I can't quite say."

"Try."

"Help me."

"Do you ever think of hurting yourself?"

"Don't be infantile. Do you mean do I ever think of killing myself? No, I don't."

"Talk about *that.*"

"What do you mean? Talk about what? I don't think of committing suicide. I'm fifty-five, and sometimes I'm weary and my life is a familiar pattern to me and I can't sleep and I don't really have any friends. Except you."

"Okay, so tell *me* how you feel."

"I have. I *am*. I have, as Hamlet put it, lost all my mirth."

"Were you happier in the past?"

"Yes, I think so. I remember that I once loved to go to the gallery, to sit there and look at the works of art. I would study them like a scholar and try to understand what the painter felt when he painted a work. What was his sorrow, his joy, his ecstasy? I thought about all that. I had a few friends then. We could talk about art, not about the fashion of the moment, of the year, but about the beauty of it, the best of it. They moved away, got out of the business, left New York. Perhaps I should have gotten out too, years ago."

"Do you think about that?"

"Not much anymore. I've become fatalistic. It is my gallery and I will keep it as long as there are fools who walk right by the wonderful paintings and buy the expensive terrible ones."

"That's cynical of you."

"Certainly it is. But in my present state it is the only path I can take. What would I do if I sold the gallery? Assuming I could sell it. What would I do with the money? I don't need it. I have money. Where would I go every day? I don't want to travel. I don't want to live in a mansion in one of those obscure suburbs. I don't want to run my own foundation. I don't have anyone I want to give the money to. I don't need anything I don't have."

"You must need something you don't have or you wouldn't be unhappy."

"Yes. Yes. But I don't know exactly what that is or how I can get it."

"Someone to talk to? Other than me, I mean."

"Perhaps. I try to pretend I'm not lonely. I try to keep to my schedule. It doesn't always work. Someone to talk to? Yes, someone to talk to. But who?"

"I don't know. I don't have such answers."

"I don't either. There are times when I'm in the park when I want to talk to people. I want to go up to one of the mothers at the zoo and say, 'That is a delightful child you have,' but I don't do it. I suspect that she would think I was demented. The city does that to you. A stranger walks up, and you think immediately that something bad is about to happen.

"I watched a young boy, maybe fourteen, walk up to an older woman at the Seventy-second Street entrance to the park on Fifth Avenue. I couldn't hear what he was saying, but he must have been saying something pleasant, because the woman was smiling at him. Then suddenly he grabbed her purse and ran. She started to scream and she ran after him. He came right at me, a terrified look on his face. I froze. He raced by me into the park. She ran after him screaming. No one else moved. All of us, and maybe there were fifteen or twenty people around, all of us froze. Only the two of them were in motion. Bernard barked once or twice. I took him home, but I could see my heart beating through my shirt. When I got home I thought about that smile on her face when she first talked to the boy. The betrayal. The horror. And I knew again that it is a risk to talk to anyone you don't know. Yet I do try. I do."

"How?"

"Occasionally I'll be walking Bernard somewhere in the park.

We take a number of paths, but usually we walk along the mall toward the band shell. It is for me an almost pastoral place, despite the fact that you can see all those buildings on every side of the park, reminding you that you're in New York. It is a peaceful place. I'll be walking there and I'll see someone sitting on a bench or on the grass and I'll want to begin a conversation."

"Do you?"

"Rarely."

"Ever?"

"Sometimes I try to have a chat with a boy. You know, when I think of my own childhood I think that it was the happiest time in my life. We were all innocent then, without any of that terrible guile you pick up along the way. I had my mother—my father, you may recall, died when I was three—and she took care of me, lovingly, thoughtfully, wisely. My friends were good friends. We played together, all day and into the night, and we never worried about anything. Certainly we didn't worry about our loyalty to each other. When I was twelve and thirteen and fourteen, even beyond that, they were all good years."

"And now?"

"Now. It's not the same, of course, and I'm not a fool about that. I know it's never the same. I do try to talk to those boys in the park. I suppose I think they'll bring back some of that innocence, some of that honesty. Yet they've changed too. I mean that children are not as they once were. In this city they're adults, cynics, at fifteen. But I try. I talk to them."

"What happens?"

"I don't remember. Really. At times I feel idiotic. Why do I bother to talk to them? Is that what lonely people do in this city? Whatever the case, the conversations don't amount to much."

"What are you hoping for?"

"I don't know exactly. Maybe I just want to have some good talk, to tell someone else what I know."

"There's nothing wrong with that."

"No, there isn't, but they don't want to listen. We are obviously incompatible."

"So?"

"I get up and leave. I don't remember how I do it always, if I say anything snide or just get up and leave. I don't remember. I do remember that after those talks I feel depressed, queasy, almost numbed by it all. I have to get away from there. I remember later that I was sweating heavily, through my shirt, and I can smell it. Frustration, no doubt."

"No doubt. How do you feel about it now?"

"The same. 'Rejected' is the right word. I don't want to have instant friendships. I'm not mad. I look for simple conversation, but not small talk. There's always that hideous wall between us. I never seem to get to say what is in my mind. I can tell that they simply tolerate me, those boys. They see me as an old bore, a pest."

"Too bad."

"The last time, it bothered me for several days. I went back to the park a few days later and looked for him where we had sat. He wasn't there, of course. I hadn't done *that* since I was a freshman in college. I had broken up with a woman and I knew where she would be that weekend, some small town on the Jersey shore. So I got into my car and drove down there. I drove along all the streets of that town looking for her car. I thought I saw it parked in front of a small summer cottage near the beach. I pulled up and ran into the house looking for her. There were people in the house, strangers, and she wasn't there. It was the wrong house, the wrong car. I got into my car and drove back to the city."

"Will you look for him again?"

"No. I know better. Even if I found him, we'd have nothing to say to each other."

"That saddens you somehow?"

"Yes and no. I would like to talk to him, but at the same time

I know that we couldn't talk to each other for long. Not enough to say anything."

"It's time."

"Fine. We can talk about it the next time."

"Yes."

"Maybe I'll meet someone else. Maybe we'll be able to talk."

"Maybe. We'll see."

"Yes, we will."

After he left, the doctor sat behind his desk rolling a pencil in his fingers. Why does that man bore me? he thought. After all these months, why don't I have very many friendly thoughts about him? Why does he seem so dull? He wondered if he had been of any help to the man, given him any kind of real support, significant hope. He did not know the answers to any of the questions. During their sessions his mind wandered. He thought about his wife and whatever it was that she was doing to him that was turning him against her. Was his boredom with Wilton a product of his rage toward her? He couldn't solve that puzzle yet, either, but it seemed more interesting to him than that sad patient's whines. He would have to devote more time to all of it, he realized. At that instant he heard the door to the reception room open and he got up, a smile on his face, to greet the next patient. She would have vivid sexual fantasies to recite. He looked forward to them. They kept him alert.

Sunday

It was eleven A.M. and Gruber's feet ached. He had been on patrol in the park for several hours, and the tour had been so uneventful that he couldn't remember anything about it, except that his feet hurt. He stopped at the band shell and looked around; there weren't any other cops in sight. He sat down on a bench, lit a cigarette and watched the smoke hover in the hot summer air. He could feel the dampness on the back of his shirt. He hated days like this, and after almost twenty years on the force he still hadn't gotten used to walking in the summer heat. Had he been more crafty, he thought, he would be behind some desk by now instead of repeating the ritual of covering a beat day after day.

Others he had joined the force with had managed to get ahead, but in recent years they were cutting back instead of adding to the force, and they were giving many of the better jobs to blacks. Too many of his friends on the force knew how Gruber felt about "niggers"; he was convinced that he'd been punished, unofficially, for expressing his views on that touchy subject. Nevertheless there was the pension to look forward to and he didn't intend to jeopardize that now. In a few years he'd be collecting that, not compensation for all the abuse he'd taken over the years, but something to depend upon.

He rubbed his ankles. He did the work, he thought, while the

81

Captain and Fahey and the others sat at the precinct playing their roles. You could solve most of the crimes in the city, he said to himself, if you just busted everybody in Harlem. He smiled at his own sense of ingenuity, then noticed that a five-year-old boy nearby was pointing at him, calling his mother's attention to the seated policeman. Grubber got up slowly and realized that he was getting fat. Too much beer, he thought.

Now the Captain had asked for help on the Torres case from the Street Crime Unit and had come up with a young nigger cop who stood around and waited for someone else to solve it for him. A dumb move, Gruber thought, because in this case they were certainly looking for a nigger maniac, and one nigger wouldn't do too well at finding another. He looked around the band shell and spotted a young black he knew had sold dope to kids in the area. He felt like rushing over and pushing the kid around, just to plant some fear in him, but if he did he might actually find some dope and that would mean he'd have to bust the kid and get involved in all the paperwork required.

It was too hot for that kind of excitement, he decided. He pointed his nightstick at the kid, who spotted him and began to move away, edging out of reach. Gruber was warmed by that show of respect.

He resumed his walk, heading south along the mall. A few mothers were wheeling their infants. A couple of tennis players passed him heading north toward the courts. The park had not yet come alive for the day. Fortunately for Gruber, he didn't work the park at night, when it could be a horror show. He simply put in his days, one after another, working toward that pension.

As he walked south down the mall, he spotted a black kid asleep on an otherwise empty patch of grass on the west side of the mall. He hated that, kids who came to the park to sleep, kids who did nothing with their time. This black kid would get a scare, Gruber decided.

He walked over to the kid, who was wearing a white T-shirt and old jeans and battered sneakers. The T-shirt had a red circle on the front of it. Like a Jap flag from World War II, Gruber thought, until he got closer and realized that the spot was a large bloodstain.

He leaned over the boy, said "You okay?" and knew the answer. Blood continued to ooze from that single entry wound over the heart and the stain was spreading.

"Mary, mother of God," Gruber said. Two passing bicyclists stopped nearby. "Keep going," Gruber shouted. He took out his walkie-talkie and called for aid, then went through the boy's pockets for identification.

He found an old playground sports club card with the name Cliff Peterson on it, and an address on West 107th Street. He found a baseball card, a set of keys, two sticks of gum and six dollars in bills. He folded the bills and put them into his back pocket, keeping the rest of what he'd found in his hand.

Within minutes help arrived, and Gruber went back to the precinct to give his report.

The conclusion was immediate. Torres' killer had found a second victim. Men went out to try to find out why. They managed, at best, to reconstruct Peterson's day.

He had gone to a rock concert at the Beacon Theater on Broadway the night before with some friends. "Cliff is dead? Man, Cliff is dead?" one of them repeated like a chant while being questioned. After the concert Peterson had gone home. He had said something to his father, who had been awake and drunk, but his father couldn't remember what Peterson had said to him.

His mother had been asleep. She told detectives that if she had been awake maybe this wouldn't have happened; she had planned to take her son to visit relatives the day he was killed. She was distraught. Cliff had never been in any trouble, she said; he did not have a single enemy in the world and had never been arrested.

Apparently, judging from the unwashed dishes in the kitchen, Peterson had gotten up on Sunday, eaten a bowl of potato chips and had a Coke. He must have been out of the house by nine A.M., his mother said, because she got up at nine-thirty and he was gone.

No one saw him in the park until Gruber found his body beside the mall. He didn't have any money in his pockets when he was found, but that was because he probably hadn't had any when he left home. Robbery was not a reasonable motive, the investigators concluded.

Ballistics would have something to say about the bullet, and how it compared to the one that killed Torres. Until then, conversation at the precinct would center on the similarity between the two crimes.

Gruber was back on his beat by midafternoon, resuming his patient stroll through the park, waiting for his shift to come to an end so he could go home and catch the second game of a doubleheader on television.

Let the smart nigger solve this one, he said to himself. I'm just taking it easy. He leaned against a tree, patted his paunch, lit a cigarette and watched an attractive young woman in a bikini acquire a suntan.

Tuesday

The *Times* had run a three-paragraph story. The *News* had obtained a photo of the murder spot and had connected the two murders. Sergeant Fahey was livid. He summoned several members of the Central Park precinct to his office.

"All right. Two kids dead. The same way. One bullet each. Economical. That's all we know," he said.

"Fourth Homicide is into it. Their men are all over the park, finding nothing. We've got four of our own men, from the Anti-Crime Unit, stumbling around the park posing as drunks and cripples. Half of the force is wondering what the hell we're doing," he added, pacing in front of his desk. "The other half seems to be working on the case. If we don't figure it out soon, we're going to look like morons."

Mark Goldman squirmed in his chair. It was the toughest case he'd encountered. Homicide's men, out in the open, went around asking questions, but couldn't find anyone to provide any answers. Detectives from the precinct hunted clues—a fingerprint, a heel mark, anything—without success. As Fahey had pointed out, the precinct's own Anti-Crime men had fanned out too.

Goldman knew the four men who had been chosen. They were able, inventive, concerned. While the meeting went on in Fahey's office, they were out there. One hobbled on crutches, looking like a drunk who had fallen down and broken a leg. Another wore a crash helmet and jeans and a jean jacket, a biker looking for kicks in the park. The other two, done up in fancy clothes, strolled along in the manner of a gay couple. Goldman knew and liked them all, but he wondered if they would have any luck. He listened to Fahey.

"The Medical Examiner doesn't tell us much. Two kids murdered. We knew that. Each one killed with a single shot, and there wasn't any daylight between the barrel and the kid when the shots were fired. Ballistics is taking guesses. They figure it's a miniature weapon, like the Colt derringer. Anybody here know it? Well, it's a twenty-two and we know that's the caliber involved in these murders. We haven't found a witness. Figure that the weapon may have had a silencer attached to it.

"Any good machinist can make one. You knock off the front sight and thread the outside of the barrel. You fit a piece of threaded pipe to it. Inside that pipe there's another metal tube. Its interior dimension matches the bore diameter of the weapon. You drill holes to allow the gas to escape on firing. Put in some washers, some solid, some mesh, to help muffle the sound.

"So we may be looking for a nut with a gun you can hold in the palm of your hand, a gun you can't hear. Who the hell is he? Or is she? Another kid? Some lunatic? A creep with a cause? What did the two victims have in common? They were teen-agers. Nothing else seems to link them. Nothing. But maybe that's *something*. Who kills teen-agers? Other teen-agers maybe. But with a rare kind of weapon and a silencer? Not likely. So who are we looking for? I haven't a fucking idea." Fahey seemed more agitated. He kicked his desk, pounded it with both hands simultaneously.

"You know the Colt derringer? The barrel pivots so you can insert one bullet. Just one at a time. If you miss with it you're in trouble. This guy hasn't missed yet."

"What do you think?" Goldman asked Fahey.

"How the hell do I know *what* to think? We've got some of our best men out there. If they tell me something, anything, maybe I'll know what to think. Right now I'm sure of just one thing. We've got two murders to account for, and unless I'm bananas we'll probably have a third soon, unless we stumble on a freak loading a Colt derringer in the middle of the zoo. Don't count on that. Be alert, for Christ's sake. Don't loaf. Keep looking around. And if you see anything that might matter, note it."

The men filed out of his office. Jackson lingered.

"Ever had anything like this before?" Jackson asked Fahey.

"A couple of times. But you're never ready for it," Fahey said. "It's always bad when they're knocking off kids."

"Did you get anything from the kids' parents?"

"Nothing but grief. First you tell them that their son has been killed. Then you're supposed to say, 'Pardon me, can you help me collect clues?' They're falling apart and you stand there and try to get some information. Sure we tried, but in these cases they didn't have anything to give us. Zero."

"I'm trying," Jackson said. "But I don't know what I'm looking for. Yet. Maybe soon I will."

"Keep looking, for God's sake," Fahey said. "The less I see of you around here, the better I'll feel."

Jackson shrugged and headed for the door to resume his quest in the park.

Thursday

It was hot by noon. Samuels had enough money for food for three and one admission to a movie. Markham and Morgan joined him for hamburgers, french fries and Cokes at an east side coffee shop, then Samuels led the way along East 72nd Street.

Markham and Morgan trailed a half block behind Samuels. At the theater Samuels confidently stepped up to the box office. Morgan, out of the ticket seller's sight, turned to Markham: "What is this movie all about, man? *A Man and a Woman.*"

"I think it's porn," Markham answered.

"Will they sell a ticket to John?"

"Sure. He looks old, man."

Samuels bought one ticket and went into the theater. Morgan and Markham sauntered past the ticket booth and waited. Samuels, once in the theater, raced down the aisle past the empty seats and opened the exit door, blocking the lock with a book of matches.

Morgan dashed down the alleyway next to the theater; Markham followed. They slipped into the theater and searched for Samuels in the darkness. Spotting a cigarette glowing in the balcony, they ran up the stairs and sat down beside Samuels.

"Good work, man," Morgan said.

"Uh," Markham grunted.

"What's the flick about?" Morgan asked.

"I don't know," Samuels said, "but it's three-for-one day, and that makes it worthwhile."

"We'll see," Morgan said.

A few other patrons entered the theater, but no one joined them in the balcony. Within a few minutes the film began.

"Oh, shit," Morgan said. "It's in French."

"I know a little French," Markham volunteered.

"Forget it," Samuels said. "Just enjoy it."

Markham fell asleep. Morgan puffed on a cigarette furiously, in frustration. Samuels tried to concentrate on the film. It had to do with a woman whose husband had been killed and a guy without a wife and how the two of them managed to get it on, but he couldn't cut through the language or the subtitles to manage a complete understanding. He grew restless.

"You said it was porn," Morgan said to Markham.

"I was wrong," Markham said, awakening.

"Don't do it again, man," Morgan said. "I was all set to dig it."

"Sure," Markham agreed.

Someone in the darkness below turned around and hissed at them. Morgan hissed back.

"Don't be rude," Samuels said.

"Rude! Rude? What am I doin' at this flick?" Morgan snapped.

"You are in for free," Markham said. "Relax."

"This ain't my kind of movie, man," Morgan said.

"Okay, okay." Samuels sighed. "Let's go."

The three got up and made their way toward the main stairway, out of the theater and into the sunlight.

"I hate to come out into the sun," Markham said. "You should go to movies at night, so you always come out into the dark. It's too weird to come out during the day."

"I'll think about that," Samuels said.

They walked west on 72nd Street, toward the park, in silent agreement, and entered it, slouching and quiet, uncertain of their plans for the rest of the day.

"Excuse me." A man's voice interrupted their walk. "Can you tell me the correct time?"

"No," Morgan said, still annoyed by the film, "I ain't got no watch."

"It's almost four," Samuels said, looking at his watch.

"Thank you," the man said, leading his dog toward Fifth Avenue.

They walked to the Bethesda Fountain and sat on the edge of it, dipping their hands into the water.

"Hey, isn't that the cat who just asked you for the time?" Morgan said to Samuels.

"Yes," Samuels said, staring at the man approaching the fountain. "Sure is."

"Wasn't he heading toward Fifth?" Markham asked.

"Seems he was," Samuels said. "Guess his dog didn't do his thing yet."

"To the shell, men," Morgan shouted, bounding up.

They walked up the stairs, across the transverse and into the band-shell area.

"Want some coke?" A tall black teen-ager was holding a small packet in his hand.

"How about a Fresca, baby?" Morgan asked.

"You go fuck yourself," the black teen-ager said. "You just do that."

"If I could, man, I would. Yes, I would," Morgan shouted.

They sat on one of the empty benches facing the band shell.

"What'll we do now?" Markham asked.

"Don't know," Samuels said.

"How about we climb up on the shell and sit on top and just dig what's happenin'?" Morgan suggested.

"Too hot. Too hot up there now. Later. In the cool of the evening," Samuels said.

"My mother says we should be careful," Markham said.

"Tell her we will be," Samuels answered.

Friday

Wilton was restless. He crossed and uncrossed his legs, clenched and unclenched his fists.

"What is it?" the doctor asked.

"What is it?" Wilton repeated softly. "I don't know. I am fifty-five. I am of average height, average weight, as they say. I feel anonymous."

"Lonely, you mean?" the doctor asked.

"Yes, I suppose so. There is so little to do, if you know what I mean."

"Uh-huh."

"Uh-*huh.*" Wilton stressed the second syllable. "Why do you say that? Uh-huh. It is like the sound of a bell that tolls without feeling as I tell each chapter of my story."

"Don't be melodramatic. I meant 'yes.' "

"Then say 'yes.' "

"I'll try."

" 'Yes' means something. 'Uh-huh' means nothing."

"All right."

"Yes, I'm still feeling lonely. There aren't any women in my life. I don't want any. There aren't any men in it either. I feel alone when I work and I feel alone when I'm at home. I have Bernard, my dog. It isn't enough. I eat my meals alone."

"Surely you *do* something."

"I have my soldier collection."

"And your gun. You could start an army."

"Don't be funny."

"I'm sorry."

"I just bought several marvelous porcelains from France. Nine inches tall. Two hundred and seventy-five dollars each. Magnificent."

"What makes them special?"

"They are perfect. Their weapons are cast in metal, their belts and straps are real leather, their banners cloth. They are splendid."

"What others do you have?"

"Do you know anything about them? I've forgotten."

"No."

"Some of them are antiques. Names like Courtenay, Mignots, Lineols, Heyde. Years ago they were sold for two dollars for a set of eight, say in 1914. Now, I pay three hundred for them, for eight of the King's African Rifles. The others are Bavarian cavalry or court figures, perfect little court figures, knights. They are remarkable. Beautiful."

"So you have them, the soldiers, and Bernard. You are not totally isolated."

"The soldiers do not speak. Bernard does not speak, although he tries to make himself understood. They are not companions."

"You want a companion?"

"Of course. Don't you?"

"We're not talking about me."

"Correct. We're talking about *me*. We have been for months, haven't we?"

"Uh-huh. *Yes.*"

"Yes."

"I thought about that this morning, how many months you've been coming to see me. Why is it that you never call me by name?"

"What do you mean?"

"I mean by name. You never use my name or call me 'doctor.' "

"I hadn't thought about it, to be honest. I don't know whether I think of you as 'doctor' or as 'Abraham' or as 'Abe' or as 'Doctor Weinstein' or whatever."

"Isn't that a bit odd? That you shouldn't have a way of referring to me?"

"Perhaps. But I do keep coming, don't I? I am a loyal patient, one of the most loyal you have, certainly. I am here in rain or snow, in heat waves and blizzards, telling you my endlessly dull story month after month. We will grow old together, won't we?"

"Are we friends?"

"I don't know. Do you want me to be your friend or your patient?"

"You are my patient, of course. I wondered how you felt about it."

"I don't know how I feel about it. I do know that I arrive here several times a week and we wonder together about my fate. I pay for that. And you listen. Does that definition offend you?"

"I don't know. I want to think about it."

"Well, think about it. As for me, I want to coexist somehow with the rest of the world, without feeling an invisible pain. I go to the park often, several times a day, because it reminds me of my childhood, of the happiness I had in parks. Yet I know that the park can be dangerous. People get killed there. Have you read the *Times* lately?"

"I don't read the *Times.*"

"The *Daily News?*"

"I don't read the newspapers."

"I see. You aren't missing much. There have been some murders in the park, however. Unsolved, motiveless murders. Young boys."

"Hasn't that always been the case in the park?"

"I suppose. But I worry about myself more these days. And what is odd is that I have the feeling that I knew the victims."

"Knew them? How?"

"I don't know. It reminds me of my grandfather. After my grandmother died, he began to believe that he had known all sorts of people he'd never known. Famous people. Obscure people. He hadn't known any of them, of course. Sometimes I read the *Times,* about these awful things, and I think I knew them somehow. I don't know *how,* exactly. I simply think it."

"I haven't kept in touch with life in the park. I have so many professional papers to read, it is difficult to be loyal to the *Times.*"

"Of course."

"How do you feel physically?"

"Not badly. I am careful about that. I still have some pride. I walk a great deal and that keeps me trim. I choose my clothes with care. I spend little these days on anything else."

"I've always thought of you as well dressed."

"So have I. It costs more to be well dressed these days, but I have the money. When I see something I think is handsome, I buy it. It is my self-indulgence."

"Fine. There's nothing wrong with that."

"I have this extraordinary leather shoulder case. Magnificent leather. I've taken to carrying that little gun in it, for protection."

"Isn't that an illusion?"

"Probably."

"I mean it is almost a toy gun, isn't it? I remember your description of it. Sounded like an antique. Why carry that around? Or any gun, for that matter?"

"I've told you. Terrible things go on in this city. I don't want to die that way, murdered by some cretin in a dark corner of the park."

"Do you think about death?"

"At times. I cannot deal with the thought. You might think that I would welcome it. But I don't. I am not ready for it."

"It is difficult to be ready for it."

"Obviously. And yet at times when I'm in the park walking

Bernard I suddenly feel numb. It may go on for minutes. Numb. And my hearing seems to be affected. I don't hear anything. I feel hot, frighteningly hot, not the heat of the day. Later, when I'm home and am feeling better, I wonder if that is how death prepares us for the inevitable, by giving us some signs first, samples of a reality we cannot understand."

"I don't know."

"I don't either."

The doctor glanced at his watch. "Almost time," he said.

"Almost time," Wilton chanted.

"What can you do to combat that loneliness?" the doctor asked.

"Not a fair question at the end of the session," Wilton replied.

"Probably not. But think about it. There may be something you can do."

"Maybe there is," Wilton said wistfully. "But I haven't unearthed it yet."

"Try."

"Yes. Try."

He got up from his chair and walked out the door. The woman he often saw in the waiting room was there, reading *Cosmopolitan* again. He looked at her without smiling, went out the door and into the street.

The doctor asked the woman to come into his office. He closed the door to his office, thinking about Wilton. Something, he thought, is troubling Wilton more than ever. He didn't know what it was. He would have to think about it after dinner tonight. Then he thought about dinner and the fantasy returned: his wife would stop being aloof and she would seduce him before dinner. He considered the details of that scene and forgot about Wilton.

Wilton returned to the gallery. He picked up an art magazine, grew weary of it, put it down. The front door opened and a tall patrician woman entered. Long dark brown hair carefully done. Eyes, mouth, face all meticulously made up. Expensive clothes in muted colors. Wilton moved forward to greet her.

"May I help you?" he asked. He disliked the expression, the implication of menial service, but it was the easiest way to begin a dignified negotiation.

"Perhaps," she said. "I'll browse."

He returned to his desk and studied her as she moved slowly from one work to another in long graceful strides.

She turned toward him and said, "I know something about art. But if you have a special piece you're hiding, I wouldn't know that. What you have out here isn't for me. Is there something that might be?"

Crafty, he thought, shrewd. He didn't care about her knowledge of art; he was fascinated by her. There was a coolness about her that intrigued him.

"I have nothing for sale that you cannot see, except a few minor works I am not yet interested in selling."

"I see." She smiled at him, directly at him. "But I don't believe you. You couldn't exist in this gallery selling what you show. There must be more."

Too crafty, he thought. Why was she trying to provoke him?

"You are saying that you buy only first-rate art?"

"I am," she said.

"Why not come back in two weeks? I may have a gem or two for you then," he said, thinking that he might produce them from his private stock for her.

"Why not now?" she asked.

He considered it, but he was beginning to feel manipulated by her beauty. It had not happened in a very long time. He resisted.

"Not now. Perhaps in a few weeks."

"Well . . ." She sighed, moving toward the door.

He didn't want her to leave. "Why don't you come back at six?" he asked. "We could have drinks, or dinner, and talk about my strange attitude about selling art."

"No. I don't think so," she said. "But I may be back." She waved gently and left.

She won't be back, he said to himself. He wondered if his conversation had been banal or inept. He wondered why he could not persuade her to have a drink with him. He slumped in his chair behind his desk and stared at the door.

Jackson listened politely to the Captain of the Central Park precinct. It was, he felt, the proper thing to do, although he already knew much of what the Captain had to tell him about the two murders. It was important to show his respect.

The Captain, a large, round, bald veteran of the force named Jorgensen, had never had a job outside the police department. He had dealt with most of the crimes known to the force in the four decades he had spent on it. In one year at the Central Park precinct he had witnessed a procession of crimes almost comparable to what he had surveyed in his entire previous duty.

"You know what this fucking park is?" he asked Jackson. "It's a fucking Calcutta."

"I know," Jackson said.

"You don't know. You're a kid, a kid. Before I got here I thought I'd seen every fucking kind of horror we can see. Severed heads. An arm in a trash can. Babies scalded to death. All of it. You know what? This park is the worst."

"I've heard it's getting worse," Jackson said.

"I can't tell. It's bad, always bad. Take yesterday. I got every guy I can spare looking for a murderer we don't know anything about. Meanwhile, two Ricans assault a pregnant woman in daylight. Some fucking goof from Trinidad cuts up his own kid in the Sheep Meadow. A nut from Jersey takes a trip to the zoo and tries to poison a deer. Poison a deer, I said. A pretzel vendor goes crazy and hits one of my men. What the Jews call *chutzpah*, right? One of them proper east side college girls stumbles in to tell us that she saw a guy with a hard-on hanging out of his pants. Can she identify the guy? No. Can she identify the hard-on? Don't ask. Even if we didn't have these murders, I could use you. I could use any help I can get. I don't know if you're any good or not, but

105

I'm glad you're around. There are too few cops working today. I'm making a fucking speech."

"It's okay. You've got to be pragmatic about the human condition."

"You talk funny."

"What do you mean I talk funny."

"I mean you talk funny. I can't explain."

"You mean I'm black but I don't talk black?"

"Maybe. I don't know what I mean. I don't know what I'm doing half the time, things have gotten so crazy around here. Whatever I mean, forget it. If all the guys I've got in the bushes out there—looking for God knows what—can't figure out these murders, maybe you can."

"Maybe. But don't count on it. We don't seem to have much to go on, do we?"

"Next to nothing." Jorgensen sighed, leaning back in his chair. He resumed talking, but Jackson wasn't listening.

Mary, Mary, what am I going to do about you? he asked himself. He thought about her body. He often thought about her body and he had to concentrate in order to stop thinking about her body. The case, the case. He imagined a faceless man shooting a teen-age boy and walking away calmly while other people simply walked by. He remembered the way Mary's breast felt, smooth, in his hand and he began thinking about her again. He needed her body and he knew that was sexist and he tried to see more to it than that. He knew there was more, but right now he could only think of her hips and her waist and her mouth. He tried again to get back to the case. And he thought about Mary. Soon he would have to solve that riddle, the attraction she represented and the values she promoted to him, values he couldn't adopt. Her body appeared again in his reverie and he appreciated it.

"Do you know that? Do you know it?" Jorgensen was yelling.

"What? Do I know what?" Jackson said.

"Every time I pick up my phone some son of a bitch tells me

I've got to solve this. I tell 'em that's why I joined the fucking force in the first place, way back when we had horse-drawn wagons. To *do* something."

"And if you don't there'll be a commission to investigate why you didn't and a commission to investigate the commission and you'll be doing community work in the South Bronx until you retire."

"Not exactly. But be a good boy and go out there and take care of this for me, please."

"I will not think of myself as a loyal member of the force— tireless, intelligent and crafty—but as your son, a son of another color, home to help you through your golden years."

"Thank you, my son."

"Everybody at the precinct knows who I am, right? They've seen my face?"

"Right. If you're lucky, one of my men won't take a shot at you if he sees you talking to some kids. We won't keep track of you, either, so keep track of yourself and keep in touch with us."

"That seems reasonable, and—" Jackson turned toward the sound of pounding on the Captain's door. The Captain stood up as Sergeant Fahey came in.

"We got a guy out here says he did both," Fahey said.

"Did both what?" the Captain asked.

"Did both murders—Torres and Peterson."

The Captain nodded toward Jackson. "See him," he ordered.

Jackson followed Fahey out the door into another room.

The man was in his late thirties or early forties and was immaculate, wearing a pair of new Bally loafers, expensive slacks and an Yves St. Laurent print shirt. He seemed distracted as he stared into space, ignoring Jackson.

"Yes?" Jackson said, pulling a chair beside the man's and sitting down.

"Yes," the man repeated.

"What's your name?"

"Oliver."

107

"Oliver what?"

"Parker. Oliver Parker."

"Where do you live?"

"On Park Avenue, in the seventies."

"Alone?"

"No. With my wife."

"You come to the park often?"

"Frequently. Yes."

"Do you work?"

"No. I have money."

"I see." Jackson got up and began pacing slowly in front of Parker.

"I killed them both," Parker said. "They were disreputable."

"Disreputable? How?"

"Sloppy kids who hang around the park. There are thousands of them. They put their graffiti everywhere. They use foul language. They offend women. I hate them."

"You know you can have a lawyer with you now and that you don't have to tell me anything," Jackson said.

"Certainly. There is no point in observing the rules, however. I am guilty."

"Guilty of what?"

"Murder."

"Tell me about it."

"There isn't all that much to tell. I killed them both."

"How?"

"I recognized them both as the worst sort of human being. One needn't be too perceptive to seize that truth. I engaged them in conversation where we wouldn't be seen. Then I stabbed each one once, put the knife in my pocket and walked away."

"And you couldn't endure the guilt so you turned yourself in?"

"Precisely."

"Thank you," Jackson said, walking out of the room. Fahey was waiting for him.

"Well?" Fahey asked.

"Well nothing," Jackson said. "Don't waste time with confessions like that one. The guy's a borderline case. If you call his wife and tell her he's here, she may not be shocked. Tell her to get his therapist involved right away. You can bet he's got one, because he's loony—but not loony enough—and because he's self-absorbed and has money. He reads the papers; that's how he knew something about the murders. But he doesn't read carefully. Those boys were shot and he sat there and told me how he stabbed them. Send him home."

"Shit," Fahey grunted.

Jackson returned to the Captain's office.

"So?" Jorgensen asked.

"Zero."

"Of course. If I had good luck I wouldn't be in this job in this place at this time. Right? The guy who killed those kids isn't going to come walking into the station to tell us that he did it and how he did it. Right? Right. He's going to keep on doing it and I'm going to have to start taking medication for high blood pressure and I could go at any minute, before you, single-handed, find the guy."

"Who says it is a guy?" Jackson asked.

"Well, it could be an enraged zebra. What do you mean 'Who says it is a guy?'"

"I mean it could be a woman, couldn't it?"

"Never. Not a chance. I feel that in my gut."

"Is your gut reliable?"

"Most of the time."

"Okay. I'll respect it until further notice. We are looking for a guy. Young? Old? Short? Tall? Skinny? Fat? Alone or with someone?"

"Why are you asking me those questions? Are you trying to depress me?"

"Of course not. I respect the delicate nature of your health."

"Never mind my health. Worry about the health of all those kids who are playing out there, or smoking dope or tinkering with their tools in the bushes. I don't want to lose another of them. Understand?"

"Understand. And after I have a well-balanced lunch I intend to take a long attentive stroll through our beloved green. My eyes will be open at all times, not to mention my ears. Trust me and perhaps my good luck will improve yours."

"You talk funny."

"Right on, baby," Jackson said, smiling. He left the Captain's office and walked into the hot air of summer, alert, confident and baffled.

Warren Jackson had spent several evenings reading books about Central Park. He did not know what he was looking for, exactly, or if there was anything he might find that would be useful to him. He did want to know the park; although he had spent many days in it, he didn't know its geography as well as he wanted to. He discovered that the Tavern-on-the-Green, across the road from the Sheep Meadow, was originally designed to house the sheep that grazed on the meadow, and their shepherd. He learned that the sheep had been there until 1934, when they were banished to Prospect Park on their way to elimination. He noted that some of the schist in Central Park contained gold, both real and fool's, but not enough of either to excite any prospector. What he did not learn was how the murderer he was after got into the park, managed to kill and get out without being seen and remembered.

Jackson began to walk. On hot day after hot day (it was one of New York's most torrid summers) he walked. On one day he walked along the western edge of the park, from Columbus Circle to 110th Street. He repeated the exercise on Fifth Avenue, bordering the park from Grand Army Plaza to 110th. He walked east to west and west to east along the various transverse paths.

He walked around the lake and the reservoir. He strolled around the zoo, looking for a lead, a clue. He circled the carousel and sat beside the pond. He joined a young mother and her son to get into the children's zoo. He lounged beside the mall and sat in front of the band shell. He pretended to sleep on the Great Lawn, beside its small lake. He watched softball games and picnics. He sat on a bench and saw homosexuals saunter through the Ramble. He watched dozens of New Yorkers play tennis. He leaned against a tree and surveyed the North Meadow, then walked along the Harlem Meer, watching the boats and the people in them.

He sweated heavily, and found nothing.

He grew increasingly surly. His fondness for Mary, which had been more than sexual and slightly less than love, turned to ambivalence. He began to see her insinuations, her interrogations, as provocation.

He had heard one of his fellow cops say, "A nigger did it. I can tell," and he mentioned it to Mary.

"Why do you put up with that?" she screamed.

"It is a part of it all, of being alive," he said.

"It is a part of that goddamned rotten job," she snapped. "You earn nothing. You're abused. You work day and night. You're too smart for that. Jesus, Warren, get out. Get out." She waved her arms in the air and turned her head away.

"And do what?" he asked.

"Anything respectable. Anything with a chance to make it. Make it, Warren. Make it. You're not a fool. You could make it in my business. You think. You're not another dumb nigger, destined to suffer. You've got something going for you. So don't piss it away. *Please.*"

"Are you telling me that if I quit the force and get a fat job in some ad agency—doing God knows what—that you'll love me?"

"No. I'm not saying that. We're on the verge of something, the two of us, maybe. But we're not there. And it irritates me that you can't see how much you're worth."

"Bullshit. You just can't say that you care about a guy who's a cop. That's what it is. You can't tell your chic friends about me. You have to apologize when you do, and that humiliates you.

You'd like to say that your man is making it, as fast as hell, and you're proud of that. Well, I'm not interested in making it. I don't need that much money to feel good. I need a woman, sure, a woman who cares about me and who even cares for me, who takes care of me. I need the kind of self-respect you have when you do anything well. I don't put down a carpenter who does beautiful work, just because he doesn't live in his own brownstone. I'm a cop. That's what I am. Deal with that. Don't treat me like a big lump of Silly Putty."

"You must think I'm some kind of bitch," she said, sighing.

"I'm not sure I know who you are. You're good in bed and you're smart and you know how to move all around this city. I can take you *anywhere*. That old joke. But lately you've been leaning on me, and I've about had all the leaning I can take. I'm out there sweating my ass off, trying to find somebody who kills kids. And then I come to you and I get grilled by you about my lack of desire to make it."

"I'm trying to give you good advice," she said.

"Why not just see me as me? And deal with that," he countered.

"It's hard for me. Maybe it's hard because I do care about you."

"Maybe you don't care enough," he said.

"Maybe. We'll find out."

She poured two glasses of wine and they sipped in silence. He lit a cigarette. She did too. They puffed and sipped without saying anything. It was almost midnight, and Jackson had forgotten the splendid meal she'd made and the gentle affection they had exchanged.

She didn't want the silence to continue. "How is the case going?" she asked.

"Terrible. Absolutely terrible. You know what they say to us? That more than a third of the homicides in this city are unsolved if they're not solved within two weeks. How do you think that makes me feel? Nervous. Very, very nervous. I've walked and walked and kept my eyes open and I've found nothing. Nothing."

"What will you do if you do find something?"

"I don't know. You never know until you find it."

"If you found the guy, what would you do? I mean if you really found him, face to face."

"I don't know. But I'll tell you—and I wouldn't tell anyone else."

"What?"

"I've never fired a weapon at anyone."

"Does that mean you might miss?"

"Worse."

"What do you mean?"

"It means I might not miss."

"And that bothers you?"

"I've never killed anyone. I've seen dead men and women and kids. But I've never done it."

"Could you?"

"We may find out. Soon."

They lapsed into silence again.

"Let's go to sleep," she said.

"To bed?"

"To sleep."

"You win," he said. He put his arm around her and led her into the bedroom.

Saturday

It was Jackson's intention to walk through most, if not all, of Central Park, to record his impressions in his mind. He continued his hunt. The questions about the murders remained unanswered. He could not determine yet what sort of murderer acted that way. He suspected that he was dealing with a psychotic, but he wasn't certain why he felt that way. A seemingly rational man kills for vengeance or out of a grievance against society or because his anger is out of control. If the latter is the case, he will kill wildly, without much planning. In this case the killings were neat. One bullet in each body. Not a bullet in an arm or leg, or a miss. The boys did not know each other; the killer was not annihilating a family or a gang or a company. He was drawn to boys and he was killing them because they were boys. Later, he thought, a psychiatrist will explain it all. Now the man had to be caught, and that would not be easy to do, before another boy fell. Jackson knew that another would fall and he wondered when.

It was another hot afternoon, with temperatures in the nineties, and he sat on a bench in front of the band shell and watched the procession. Young lovers and old lovers and men and women with faithful dogs. One long lean black man with a monkey and one long lean woman with a cat on a leash. He admired both the woman and the cat; they moved together gracefully. He got up

117

and bought a Coke, and as he started to return to the bench he spotted a teen-age face that was familiar. He remembered talking to that boy before, when he and Mary had seen the boy being threatened by another kid with a knife.

The boy spotted Jackson. "Hey," John Samuels said.

"Hey," Jackson responded.

"What are you doing here?" Samuels asked. "Is this where you hang out too?" He seemed to bob up and down in an imaginary basketball game, simultaneously humming a Led Zeppelin tune.

"These days," Jackson said. "Are you alone?"

"No. Morgan and Markham are over there," Samuels said, pointing toward the front of the band shell. "Yo," he yelled. Morgan and Markham walked over.

"Let's talk," Jackson said to them. They walked down the mall and sat down on the grass.

"I've got a problem," Jackson said, "and I need some help."

"You a cop?" Morgan asked.

"Takes a black man to know a black man, right?" Jackson said.

"Right," Morgan agreed. "But let's just say I know cops."

"Let me tell you something, all of you. I met Samuels and I thought that's a straight kid, and you're his friends so I'm making that same assumption about you too. Got it?"

"Cool," Morgan said.

"You know my problem?" Jackson asked.

"I believe I do," Morgan said.

"What?"

Morgan hesitated. Jackson looked at the three boys and thought that, despite their evident differences, they were alike. Samuels, open, quick-witted, personable. Morgan, black, tough, streetwise. Markham, silent, trustworthy, strong. Different, Jackson thought, yet single-minded in their loyalty to one another, in their wish to share this one summer.

"They got you out here hustling your ass around looking for the dude who wasted those kids," Morgan said.

"Right," Jackson said. "And maybe my first mistake is saying

118

that to you," he added. "And maybe my second mistake is asking you to give me some help. And maybe I'll lose my job for that. My woman would love *that*. But I figure I've got to try."

"What are you trying to do?" Markham asked, breaking his customary silence.

"You want us to help you?" Samuels broke in.

"Maybe. What I want is for you three—and I'm going to trust you and don't ask me exactly why—to be alert because I'm asking you to be alert. You're here every day and you know this park and you see hundreds of people here every day. I don't want to do one of those scenes from a Western, where I deputize you. I just want you to be alert. Understand? Alert. And when you see me around here, I want you to come up and talk, just like we're doing now, but I want you to tell me what you see, if you think I ought to know about it."

"Okay," Samuels said without hesitating.

"Sure," Markham added.

"You got it, man," Morgan said. "Although I am not always on the side of the law, I dig you."

"I am flattered," Jackson said, smiling. "Now, let's all move on."

They walked back to the mall and Jackson headed south, away from the band shell. The boys went back to it.

"You believe what we just did?" Morgan asked.

"What do you mean?" Samuels asked.

"I mean, man, we just sat there with a cop we don't even know and we said we'd cooperate. Co-op-er-ate."

"Must be a good guy or we wouldn't have done it so fast," Samuels said.

"I like the guy," Markham noted.

"So I'm goin' to help that cat and we'll find the guy who's wastin' those kids and then Jackson there will bust me for smokin' a joint on the job. Beautiful, man, just beautiful."

"Have faith," Samuels said, "and thou shalt be rewarded."

"You mean there's bread in this?" Morgan asked.

"There is more than bread. There is glory."

"Shit," Morgan muttered. "Let's go to a movie."

"No money," Markham said.

"Not enough," Samuels added.

"Shit," Morgan repeated.

They sat in front of the band shell basking uncomfortably in the heat of the day.

Sunday

Rodney Segal awoke under a tree in the park. His back ached. As his head cleared slowly, he remembered how he had gotten there, and more.

His father, a successful gynecologist, had divorced his mother six years ago and promptly remarried. With the proceeds from his lucrative practice he had bought five brownstones in Brooklyn Heights, a house in Palm Beach and a villa in the south of France. He lived in one of the brownstones, with his new young wife and their new small children, and he didn't want Rodney around reminding him of that marriage, that part of his past.

Rodney's mother lived alone in a Greenwich Village apartment and sustained herself on money she got, sporadically, from her ex-husband—and drink. Rodney preferred her to his father, but when she was drunk he couldn't get along with her. Calm conversation escalated to vituperation; debate became rage. An attractive, if decayed, woman in her forties, she would invite the men she met in bars to her apartment. She didn't want Rodney around at those times. In fact, Rodney had concluded that she didn't want him around at all.

It was Rodney's intention to hold out, to survive for two more years, when he would be eighteen and could either go away to college, if his father would pay, or simply leave New York, desti-

123

nation to be determined. Holding out, however, was proving to be difficult.

Last night he had visited his father and asked for money for a place to stay. His father had denied him the money ("You don't deserve it, the way you treat us") and refused to give him a set of keys to the apartment ("I don't want you around here smoking and playing those rock records when we're not around to watch you"). They were going away for the weekend and didn't want Rodney alone in the house. Rodney told him to "go fuck yourself," and left, slamming doors behind him.

He had gone to his mother's, where he usually stayed, only to discover that she was drunk, incapable of talking with him. She had ordered him out, said she wanted to be alone. "Up your ass," he had screamed at her. "Where the fuck am I gonna stay tonight?" She didn't answer.

He had some small change and made a few phone calls from a public telephone. He called one of the members of the band in which he played, a rock group of high school students. The guy was out of town, his mother said. He called several other friends; he had made friends at the various private and public schools he had attended in recent years (he changed from one to another almost every year). No luck.

By eleven P.M. he was out of money and out of hope of finding a place to sleep. He walked into the park and lingered at the band shell looking for one of his friends who was known to hang out there. Everyone, it seemed, had gone home.

Rodney walked along the mall and sat beneath a tree. There were a few people in the park, walking dogs, chatting, sauntering without a destination in mind. They didn't bother Rodney. He leaned against the tree and considered his alternatives.

He could call the father of a friend, another divorced father who lived alone, but he didn't know the man well enough to demand a bed for the night. He could call his mother again and hope that she had sobered up; it was not likely. Then he realized

124

that he didn't have any money. He could walk down to his mother's apartment, a long walk, in the hope that she'd take him in if he seemed exhausted. Not likely, he concluded. He'd tried that before. She would slam the door in his face or tell him how he had disgraced her. He never understood that.

He was not, after all, a criminal. He hadn't done well in school; he knew that. But that hardly seemed to make him an outcast. Obviously, in his mother's mind it had. She objected to the graffiti he inscribed on buses, trucks and walls, especially to the one he'd done on the front of her building. She had demanded that he wash it off. He had refused. The friends he had made seemed to like him, he thought, but somehow it was difficult to depend upon them.

It was difficult to be patient. He wanted to be an artist—not a graffiti artist but a genuine one—and to be able to travel around the world making a living by selling his paintings. One of the many art instructors he'd had had told him he was talented. He believed it, and when some of his friends saw some samples they expressed admiration for the precise detail and the realistic look of his work.

He didn't know how that would come to pass. Right now his problem was immediate. No place to go. Tomorrow, perhaps, he would reach some reconciliation with his father or his mother, or both. It was not likely, but it was possible. It had happened before, when he went to them feigning contrition. It had seemed to him, without a trace of self-pity, that each of them had found some separate existence, shielded from him, and that neither one really wanted him around. Originally, when he first perceived this, he told them that he felt homeless, but when that failed to elicit a response, he came to accept it. He would bide his time, establishing truces with them when that was essential and making his own way when they would not support him. Eventually, he realized, he would have to make it on his own, and that meant getting through high school first. Two more years. He would try.

Last night, however, his options had been down to one, staying in the park, and this morning, still tired and aching, he thought about that.

He felt damp and dirty, in need of a shower and a good breakfast. If he walked to the Village, he might get both at his mother's, unless she had a man in her bed and still felt bitter about their last confrontation. It wasn't worth the walk, he decided. It wasn't worth trying to sneak onto the subway, either. The last time he'd tried that he'd been caught and his mother had gotten violent about it, because she had to talk to the police about her son's mischief.

So Rodney sat on the grass and tried to figure out what to do. It was nine A.M.

He saw the dog first, a fluffy, friendly chow. It bounded up to him and began sniffing his shoes. Rodney petted it gently. Dogs never gave him any trouble. He looked up and saw the man. Respectable-looking, Rodney thought immediately.

"Hello," he said.

"Hello," the man answered, smiling. "What are you doing here?"

"I slept here last night," Rodney said, almost boasting.

"Why?"

"It seemed like a good idea," Rodney said.

"No place else to go, you mean?" the man asked.

"I guess that's it."

"Why?"

"A long story."

"Tell it," the man said, sitting on the grass beside Rodney, but placing a large handkerchief beneath him first. The man appeared to be friendly.

"Well, it's like this, man. My father hates me and my mother isn't sober enough to like me."

The man's expression changed, becoming grim. "Really? That sounds horrible."

"Not exactly. You get used to it," Rodney told him. "To being alone."

"Never," the man said. "Never."

"You know something about it?"

"Yes, I do. It is not pleasant to be alone."

"Well, I have some friends. It's just that they all seem to be away today. Summer, you know."

"Yes."

"I didn't mind sleeping here. It's quiet and the grass smells good."

"I suppose."

"Someday I'm going to do a painting of this place," Rodney said, "and sell it for a bundle."

"You paint?"

"Yes."

"That's odd. I sell paintings."

"Funny. Maybe you could sell mine, make me rich and famous."

"Maybe."

"Not a chance. Who ever heard of a famous sixteen-year-old artist? And my father and mother would probably call you to tell you to quit interfering."

"Truly?"

"Truly," Rodney repeated, imitating the formal tone of the man's voice.

"Sad," the man said.

"True," Rodney said, smiling.

"You ought to come and see me," the man said.

"Where?"

"I'll write it down for you. We could talk about painting."

"Fine. But I don't have any money to get there."

The man reached into his pocket and removed a gold clip from a thick fold of bills. He took out a five-dollar bill and handed it to Rodney.

"Write the address on it. Small. So nobody refuses to cash it."

The man took out a slim gold pen and wrote on the edge of the bill, "75th and Madison," and handed it to Rodney, who put it into his pocket without looking at it.

"Thanks," he said.

"You're welcome," the man said. "That's where my art gallery is."

"Maybe I will come over," Rodney said.

"And maybe you won't?"

"Maybe I won't."

Rodney decided that he wanted to take the money and get out of there. The man was pleasant, but he couldn't talk to him for much longer. It was getting boring.

"I think I'll split," Rodney said.

"Leave?"

"Leave."

"Why? Can't we talk a bit more?"

"Not today. I really must split now."

"Wait," the man said. He slipped the leather case that was slung over his shoulder into his lap and opened it, with his back turned to Rodney. Rodney thought that the man was going to give him more money, so he hesitated before getting up. He relaxed against the tree, his back against the trunk.

"You must not leave now," the man said without raising his voice.

"What do you mean?" Rodney asked, growing impatient.

"I mean you must not leave *now.*"

Rodney noticed that the man was sweating heavily. The skin on his face looked sleek and his eyes seemed to be fixed on Rodney.

"Don't tell me what I can do," Rodney said, in irritation.

"You need a friend," the man said, tapping his forefinger against Rodney's chest lightly.

"Maybe. But you're not *it,*" Rodney said.

"I am," the man said, tapping Rodney's chest more forcefully.

"Don't bug me," Rodney said, becoming angry.

"I won't," the man said. "I must go now too."

He tapped Rodney's chest hard. Rodney heard a single popping sound, then nothing.

The man called his dog, who had been resting nearby, seized the leash, slung his case over his shoulder and very slowly made his way to the mall. He walked north, toward 72nd Street.

Rodney remained against the tree. A few feet away the clean white handkerchief covered a patch of grass. The five-dollar bill remained wadded in Rodney's pocket.

Monday

Two detectives, Holman and Marcus, took a photo of Rodney Segal and drove over to 75th and Madison. They parked their car and stopped for a cup of coffee. Holman, at fifty-three, had been through it before, the endless walking, the repetition of questions, the note-taking, the theorizing. Marcus, new to Homicide, was in his late twenties, eager, an aspiring intellectual, an alert and ambitious detective. They sipped their coffee and discussed the case.

"We've got something. Two street names on a five-dollar bill," Holman said, puffing on a cigarette.

"You smoke too much," Marcus said.

"Forget that shit," Holman snapped. "I'll ask the questions. You watch the faces. Carefully."

"What am I looking for?" Marcus asked.

"I don't know. A twitch. A split second of recognition. You're smart. You'll know."

They got up and left the restaurant and began their rounds.

They went into the branch of the Chemical Bank and asked to see the manager. He greeted them solemnly.

"I hope there won't be any conspicuous trouble," he said to Holman. "We have an extremely conservative clientele here." He turned to the line of older women at the tellers' counter.

Holman scratched his gray hair, glanced around the bank and

handed the photo of Rodney Segal to the manager.

"Ever see him?"

"No."

"You're absolutely certain."

"Absolutely."

"Want to show the picture to your other employees?"

"No. If I haven't seen him, they haven't seen him."

"I see." Holman sighed.

They left the bank and entered a nearby shoe store.

"Police," Holman said to the only salesman, showing his identification. "Ever see this kid?"

The salesman, young and extremely skinny, with long dirty black hair, tugged at his hair.

"Maybe. He looks familiar."

"Really? How familiar?" Holman asked.

"He looks exactly like my nephew."

"Is your nephew alive and well?" Holman asked.

"Of course. I saw him last night," the salesman said.

"Well, then this isn't your nephew," Holman said.

They went into a women's clothing store, a fur store, a housewares store.

Gristede's. The manager looked at the photo without any discernible reaction. A woman in her sixties, carefully selecting potatoes from a large bin, looked up. "Police? Yes, police," she said, seemingly irritated.

"Yes, police," Holman replied.

"Why are you in here when so many terrible things are going on out there?" she raged, pointing to the street.

"We're working on a case," Holman said.

"You're always working on something, but terrible things happen all the time. It is not safe to live in this city anymore. Not safe at all."

Marcus tugged at his jacket and Holman followed him out of the store.

They went into a burger joint, an antique-jewelry store, a stationery store. They walked through the Whitney Museum talking to guards, without success.

They entered an art gallery and were greeted by the owner, a cool and dapper middle-aged man.

"Is there something I can show you?" he asked.

"No. But there is something we can show you," Holman said. He handed the Segal photo to the man.

"Yes?" the man said.

"Do you know him? Have you ever met him?" Holman asked. Marcus was staring at the gallery owner.

The man held the photo in his hand and looked at it in silence for several moments while Holman surveyed the gallery and Marcus surveyed the owner.

"No," the owner said without changing the expression on his face. He handed the photo to Holman. "No."

"No what?" Holman asked. "No, you do not know him, or no, you have never met him."

"Both," the man snapped. "And you two are intruding."

"I beg your pardon," Holman said.

"I am busy."

"There's no one else in here," Holman said.

"That's irrelevant. I am busy."

"You do not know that boy?" Holman repeated.

"No I do not."

"Thank you," Holman said. He and Marcus went out into the street and got into their car.

"Weird, very weird," Marcus said.

"Not really. Just a snob, that's all. Feels superior to us. Doesn't want to be bothered. Arrogant son of a bitch. But not, I think, the target of this plodding investigation."

"I guess so," Marcus said. "Let's report in and take our lumps."

The Captain wanted to pace, but he couldn't. His office was filled. He bobbed and weaved like a heavyweight eluding an opponent, waving his arms in the air, emphasizing a point with a sharp and sudden movement of his head. Outside, the afternoon traffic hummed by through the park, lending a constant bass line to the oratory. The men were hot and dabbed their faces with their handkerchiefs, grimacing, sighing, grunting softly to avoid annoying the Captain.

His own men paid attention; they knew better than to appear to be distracted. From other commands within the force, men leaned against the office walls staring intently at the Captain. All factions were represented. Jackson and his friend Goldman stood near the door; at times the Captain seemed to be staring at them as he made his points emphatically.

"Three," he said, raising his voice. "Three. Chico Torres, Cliff Peterson. Rodney Segal." He stopped speaking and glared slowly around the room.

"Torres. A Rican who never gave anybody any trouble. Peterson. A black kid without a record or, as far as we can tell, any enemies. Now Segal. What do we know about him?"

One of the detectives began to speak. "Not much. A clean kid. Parents divorced. They both say they loved him, cared about him, took care of him."

"Do you believe them?" the Captain asked.

"No, but they didn't kill him. I talked to a couple of the kid's friends. They say his parents couldn't stand him. He bounced around from one to the other, and lately neither one seemed to want him. Bad stuff, but not even a misdemeanor. Right now they're sitting in their fancy apartments in grief. Too late."

"What the hell was he doing in the park early in the morning?" the Captain asked.

Another detective spoke. "We figure, from what his buddies tell us, that he couldn't sleep at either parent's place and he couldn't find a friend to stay with, so he camped in the park."

"Jesus," the Captain said. "So maybe they did murder him. They won't do time for it. We'll find the guy to do that. But maybe they killed the kid."

No one replied.

"Now let me tell you all a few things," the Captain resumed. "This time we've got something. One clean white handkerchief neatly spread out near the body. A five-dollar bill in the kid's pocket. With 'Seventy-fifth and Madison' written on it."

A tall black detective from Homicide waved his arms in frustration and spoke. "A clean white handkerchief. There were millions of them made last year. They're making more just like it every few seconds. We checked it out."

"Shit," the Captain mumbled.

"The five-dollar bill is another matter," the detective continued. "There are three good prints on it. But the prints aren't on record."

The Captain slammed his right fist on his desk. The room went totally silent.

"So we're talking about a guy who is as clean as that handkerchief. Never had his prints taken. Mother of God. And if he sat on that handkerchief while he figured on killing the kid, we can't tell much from that. We don't keep a file on ass prints."

One of the detectives smiled.

"Forget it," the Captain bellowed at him. The detective stopped smiling.

"What about Seventy-fifth and Madison? What the hell does that mean?" the Captain asked.

Holman, a detective from Homicide, answered. "We don't know. Yet. Eventually we may. Right now we don't know."

"Well, what the hell have you been doing?" the Captain asked.

"Stay calm, Chief," the detective said. "We went to every one of those places, with a picture of the kid. We talked to the owners of the stores, the guys behind the counters, the delivery kids at Gristede's, the guards at the Whitney. We talked to everybody who did anything in any of those places."

"And?"

"And nothing. Not one person recognized the kid. Not one."

137

"Aren't there stores on the second floor along that part of Madison?" the Captain asked.

"Yes. I forgot. We went to them too."

"Nothing?"

"Right. Nothing."

"So you stopped."

"No. We're still looking. We don't know what we're looking *for,* that's the problem. On *Kojak* they show a picture to some guy and he makes a funny face and they bust him and ten seconds later they get a confession and twenty seconds later they get a conviction. It's not like that out there on the street. We're still looking."

"Okay. Keep looking, all of you," the Captain said. "If we don't get to it soon, I'll be walking a beat in Akron."

"Never, Captain, never you in Akron," a voice said from the rear of the room.

The Captain shouted. "There's too much we don't know. We don't know if the guy who killed that kid wrote on that bill or not. People write on bills all the time. We're figuring he did write on it. Fine. Why did he do it? Did he want to meet the kid later? If he did, why did he kill him? Maybe he started out wanting to meet him, then changed his mind and forgot about writing 'Seventy-fifth and Madison' on the bill. All we've gotten out of it is a walk on Madison. And I can feel my blood pressure rising. I am under pressure, and not just from my blood. And you guys are turning into well-paid streetwalkers. What the hell am I going to do the next time the phone rings and some asshole bureaucrat tells me we don't know what the fuck we're doing? Hand you the phone?"

No one replied.

The men sensed that the meeting had ended when the Captain lapsed into silence and began to stare into space. They filed out slowly, until only the Captain and Jackson were left in the room.

"I'm going back into the park," Jackson said.

"Sure you are," the Captain said.

"I'm doing my best."

"I believe you."

"We'll get him. We'll get him."

"Yes, we will, eventually. Will he knock over another kid first?"

"I hope not. But I'm not sure."

"Do what you can."

"I will. I know a couple of kids who hang out in the park every day. I think they can help."

"Be careful. If one of them gets hurt, I never heard you tell me about it. And if one of them gets hurt, you'll be lucky to walk that beat with me in Akron."

"I know. But we'll keep an eye on them, I promise. I don't know if they'll be able to help, but I've got a feeling they could."

"Maybe. We don't have anything to go on at this minute. You do what you think will work, that's all, and let me know when you bust the guy with the gun in his hand and he tells you that he did it. And *why* he did it."

"It's hot out there," Jackson said.

"Why are you telling me that? I know it's hot out there. Get your ass out into it and bring me the son of a bitch who's been doing all this to me."

"Got it," Jackson said. "I'm going to find those kids."

"You get there first, you understand. And if anything happens, remember I didn't hear you. I'll say that what you did was 'unauthorized' and I'll bury you with it. Understand?"

"Perfectly," Jackson said. "If it works, I'm a hero. If it doesn't, I'm destroyed."

"We don't have any heroes, Jackson," the Captain said. "Don't count on that. Just go out in the sun and do what you have to do. And don't waste any time. We've lost three kids to one nut so far this summer. I don't want to know about a fourth."

"I'm going," Jackson said, walking out of the office, out of the precinct house and into the sun and the park.

In the late afternoon, Jackson jogged up Fifth Avenue along the park, working while seeming to be playing. He wanted to find

139

the three boys he'd met; it was time, after thinking about it for a week, to enlist their aid. Yet his thoughts bounded around inside his brain in conflict. He thought about Mary, about last night.

She had been quiet. He had been quiet. They had eaten dinner, watched television and gone to bed without saying much to each other. Their lovemaking had been perfunctory, and when he got up this morning he felt claustrophobic and got out of her apartment early, before eight A.M., while she got dressed and stared at him. There wasn't any overt anger, simply ennui, and he found that vaguely troubling. If it was to end, he hoped it would end as pleasantly as possible, with some sense of recognition about the nature of incompatibility.

He thought about it while he ran; he could feel the sweat making its way into the lining of his racing suit. Mary had felt that he was too much the cop, that he was a walking cliché, the cop who thought about his work even in bed. It was not true, he felt. He did not see himself as a stereotype.

He saw his work as a series of problems to solve, not something characteristically portrayed as vicious or grim or sensational. He went from case to case like an expert researcher, collecting information and interpreting that information, moving from question to answer, from confusion to resolution.

It did, at times, trouble him. A college classmate had become a doctor, and once over dinner the friend had told him that the worst deaths in a hospital were those of children. Jackson appreciated that. The case he was working on now, he thought, reminded him of that conversation and irritated him, in a way that he could not properly define. He asked the question over and over again: Who could have murdered those kids?

Somehow, however, he felt that he had arrived at that instant just prior to recognition, that moment when he could anticipate a realization without knowing what form it would take. He thought about the look that a woman might give him to promise passion ahead. Or, more appropriately, the look on the face of a criminal just before he moves to commit a crime. He had seen and recognized both. Now, as he jogged, he didn't think about those useless clues—the handkerchief and the five-dollar bill—but about a feeling he had, and had felt before. Something would happen soon, and his role would be more vividly defined for him by what happened. He bounced along Fifth Avenue and remembered—he did not know why—a quote from Pasteur: "Chance favors the prepared mind." He knew almost nothing about Pasteur and he couldn't remember where he'd heard that line before, but it seemed pertinent. He saw himself as prepared, and he hoped that chance would be cooperative.

One aspect of this case that had been discussed, but oddly had not been stressed, was the location of the three murders. It was assumed by a number of detectives on the case that the murderer roamed the park in search of victims. That generality was true, of course, Jackson thought, but he wondered if the specific locale wasn't more important. The mall.

He cut into the park itself, made his way past the children's zoo, and found himself at the south end of the mall. He stopped jogging and sat down on the grass, gazing northward.

It was a typical Monday afternoon in the park. A magician was surrounded by a cluster of parents and children. Two mimes enthralled another group. A steel-drum band sent its hollow Caribbean sound to an audience of several dozen gawkers. Pretzel vendors were having a slow day; soft drink vendors were making money. A continual procession of walkers passed by.

Chico Torres, Jackson thought, was found on the east side of the mall, murdered by a single shot. No one had heard it or witnessed the killing. Cliff Peterson was found on a grassy area on the west side of the mall, about halfway to the south from the band shell. Again a single shot, no witnesses. Rodney Segal was found under a tree along the mall, as well. It was, Jackson thought, too clear. Yet, if the murderer was psychotic, he might be too deranged to be devious. He might be doing the obvious, for him. If he did not track his victims throughout the park, if he

141

frequented an area that was familiar to him, he might have chosen the mall and might choose it again. Perhaps, Jackson thought, he might live nearby. It was an interesting notion, but it produced nothing more than a smile. He could not interview everyone who lived within walking distance of the mall. The force could not effectively cover the entire park, staking out men everywhere. There weren't enough men in the entire city to do that successfully.

Jackson concentrated on the mall and how he might survey it meticulously. Other men would help, but the murderer wasn't after adults, it seemed. His thoughts trailed off; he saw a spectacular woman in denim shorts and an almost transparent T-shirt, with nothing on under it. She jiggled along and Jackson's eyes followed her. He admired her wiggle and enjoyed his own brief fantasy. Then he got up and resumed jogging, toward the band shell.

He slowed as he got to the shell. He looked around and finally spotted the three boys. He could see Samuels, the tallest, through the crowd, and next to him were Morgan, the chubby black kid, and quiet Markham. Jackson cut through the mob and got to them. "See anything lately?" he asked, shaking Samuels' hand.

"No."

"What are we supposed to be looking *for?*" Markham asked.

"That's the riddle," Jackson said. "I don't know. Anything weird or strange or unusual. We figure we're looking for a man, an adult, who may talk to kids."

"Nothing," Samuels said. "And we're not very good at this sort of stuff."

"I'm not so sure *I* am," Jackson said.

"Man, if you're not sure, where does that leave us?" Morgan said, exhaling loudly to punctuate his declaration of futility.

"Never mind," Jackson said. "We'll all be patient and something good will come of it."

"Maybe," Samuels said.

The four walked away, led by Jackson, south along the mall. Jackson stopped and bought each boy a drink, then they resumed their walk. They cut onto the grass on the west side of the mall, past a Puerto Rican picnic.

They sat on the grass, facing one another as if they were about to play bridge, legs crossed, heads tilted forward.

Jackson spoke. "Three dead kids. All wiped out not far from where we're sitting. Each killed with a single shot. Not a sound. Not a witness. A couple of worthless clues. How's that? Now, in my head I am looking first of all for a man. I don't know what age. But he is in and out of the park regularly, I think. I don't believe that he comes in, walks up to a kid, shoots him and runs. Don't ask me why. I don't believe that. I believe he talks to them first, gets them to a spot where he won't be easily seen, and then does it. What does he say? I don't know, but whatever it is, it works. He may give them money. That works too. I don't know how old he is or what he looks like, but I do know that he talks to kids. And kills them."

"So we're supposed to figure out if some guy is talking to kids around here?" Markham asked.

"At least," Jackson said. "At the very least. Then you tell me about it. I'll be around. Or you can get me through the precinct. I want to know anything that you know."

"Makes me nervous," Markham said.

"Makes *you* nervous?" Jackson mocked. "If any of you gets a scratch out of this, I'm out of work."

"What do you mean?" Samuels asked.

"I mean I'm not really supposed to be talking to you this way. I'm not supposed to be asking for your help. If something happens, we're all in bad trouble."

"What do you mean by 'scratch'?" Samuels asked again.

"Hurt."

"Makes me *very* nervous," Samuels said. "The guy has got a gun and I've got nothing."

"Wrong," Jackson said. "You've got your good head and you can run fast."

"Okay, I can run."

"If it comes to that, you run."

"I don't run too well," Morgan said.

"Maybe you won't have to," Jackson said.

"Maybe I'll be number four, man," Morgan grunted.

"Take my word, you won't be alone out here. I wouldn't do that to you. I worry too."

They got up and walked toward the band shell. Jackson waved at them and resumed jogging. When he got to the 72nd Street transverse, he turned around. He could see Samuels, Morgan and Markham sitting side by side atop the band shell. Jackson did not know it was possible to get up there.

It was nine P.M. and still hot. Samuels, Morgan and Markham after their talk with Jackson had spent the day in the park playing Frisbee, talking with friends, eating hot dogs and drinking Cokes, comparing notes on movies they'd seen and girls they'd met. They were weary and gritty and sweaty and unwilling to go home. Curfew, imposed by parents, was midnight, and the three agreed to observe it to the minute. That left three hours to fill.

The population of the park had begun to thin out. A few couples meandered past the band shell, stopping to kiss in the rapidly lengthening shadows. Other kids laughed and ran, making their way out of the park. A few dog walkers lingered. A lone uniformed policeman ambled along the mall.

Samuels suggested that they climb back up to the upper edge of the band shell. Morgan and Markham assented in silence, a reflection of their increasing boredom with the long days of summer in the city.

They ascended in that order: Samuels, strong and quick; Morgan, chubby and awkward; Markham, husky and methodical. At the top they sat above the park peering out lethargically, unobserved as night arrived, signaled by the coming on of the streetlights. They could see people making their way to the edges of the park, back into the city. They stared ahead, each involved with his own thoughts.

At the south entrance to the park at that moment a hansom driver greeted a well-dressed man and his dog as they got into his hansom cab parked at Grand Army Plaza.

"Where to?" the old driver asked.

"Just drive through the park," the man responded, handing the driver a twenty-dollar bill.

"Fine," the driver said. "You too tired to walk the dog back home?"

"Yes," the man said.

The hansom moved into the park, the sound of the horse's hoofs clicking against the road. As the hansom approached Pilgrim Hill near 72nd Street, the driver leaned around to offer a friendly comment on the heat wave.

The hansom was empty.

The driver shrugged, lightly tapped the twenty-dollar bill folded in his shirt pocket, and urged the horse to speed up.

At ten P.M. Samuels, Morgan and Markham were still perched atop the band shell, sleepily. Their reveries were interrupted by the sound of sneakers against wood: someone coming up the side of the band shell. A few seconds later a face emerged over the edge, then a scrambling body.

"Hey, Harvey, what's happening?" Samuels asked.

Harvey Sacks, fifteen, very short and very thin, was an acquaintance. Samuels didn't spend much time with him, because he thought that Sacks was too short. Morgan didn't like him because he was too skinny. Markham objected to Sacks's withdrawn nature; Sacks didn't say much to anyone.

"Nothing," Sacks replied.

"What you doin'?" Morgan asked.

"I just did a piece on the side of the shell," Sacks said. " 'H.S.

707' in blue." He held up a can of spray paint, obviously in search of tribute. None came. Sacks sat down and joined the trio. The four stared out at the park.

"How long you been up here?" Sacks asked.

"Hours," Samuels said.

"Nothin' else to do," Markham offered.

"Oh," Sacks said.

They sat and stared out into the night. There was no breeze, and very few sounds penetrated the stillness of the air. An ambulance in the distance. The bark of a small dog, short and shrill. A laugh. Far away the throb of a drum. A bird call from somewhere in the nearby sky.

It was ten-thirty.

"Why don't we go home?" Sacks asked.

"Go," Samuels said. "It's too early for me."

"I'm thirsty," Sacks whined.

"Go get a drink of water," Samuels suggested unemotionally.

Sacks made his way down the side of the band shell and bounded to the ground. Above, the others paid no attention to him. They hadn't asked him to join them and they were not sorry that he had left. Casually, with little interest, Samuels watched Sacks walk slowly toward the water fountain, almost obscured from view by the overhanging trees.

"Wanna go?" Morgan asked.

Samuels turned toward him. "Maybe," he said.

"What's 'maybe' mean?" Markham asked.

"Maybe we should go. It's too quiet here."

"There's nothin' else to do," Markham said.

"Except go home," Morgan said.

"Too early," Samuels offered.

"How about we sit here for another half hour, then tip?" Morgan asked.

"You can tip now if you want to," Samuels answered.

"I think we should all tip together," Morgan said.

"Okay, okay. Soon," Samuels said, peering aimlessly out into the night.

"Who's Sacks talking to?" Markham said.

Samuels and Morgan turned to see. They could see Sacks at the water fountain talking to someone, a man whose face they could not identify. There was a dog with him. The dog was visible—thick, leonine, with red fluffy fur.

"Sacks is an asshole," Markham said.

"I suppose," Samuels said.

They watched Sacks from high above. He walked alongside the man and his dog to a nearby bench, where they both sat down. Samuels, Morgan and Markham stared at them as if they were watching a dull film.

The man and Sacks seemed to be talking quietly.

"Somebody he knows, probably," Samuels said.

Morgan and Markham didn't comment.

The man got up from the bench, his dog tugging at the leash, and walked briskly toward 72nd Street. Sacks remained on the bench.

The three watched from above for fifteen minutes, wondering what Sacks was doing down there.

"Why is he just sitting there?" Samuels asked.

"Hey, Harvey," Morgan yelled.

Sacks didn't move.

"Jesus," Samuels bellowed. He began to crawl down the side of the band shell, followed by the others, making the last leap to the ground simultaneously. They raced toward Sacks, cutting along the edge of the rows of seats in front of the shell. They got to Sacks.

"My God." Samuels exhaled audibly.

There was a rapidly expanding stain, red, on the front of Sacks's T-shirt. His eyes were open but were not moving. His mouth was slightly open, but he did not speak.

"My God," Samuels yelled. Morgan had stepped back; he had

147

never seen such a sight before. Markham was frozen in his tracks several yards away.

The sound of running distracted the three boys; they turned toward the mall. Someone was running toward them. For a split second their fear made them want to run, out of the park, away from Sacks. Then Samuels recognized the runner.

It was Jackson. "Jesus," he said. "I didn't see him. I didn't hear anything. I was watching the three of you." He leaned over Sacks. "You know him?" he asked.

"Yeah," Samuels said. "He was with us up there, and he said he was thirsty, so he went for a drink of water. For a drink of water."

"God," Markham muttered.

"Man," Morgan said, his hands shaking, his head jerking almost involuntarily from side to side.

"Where were you?" Samuels asked Jackson.

"Down there, halfway down the mall. Waiting. The wrong place to wait. Jesus."

A couple walked up. They seemed to be the only other people around. "What happened?" the man asked.

"Nothing. The boy's been hurt," Jackson said. "Go home."

The couple moved away briskly.

"Who is he?" Jackson asked.

"Harvey Sacks. He's fifteen," Samuels said.

"Did you guys see anything? Anything?"

"He said he was thirsty. He crawled down and went to the fountain. He started to talk to some man."

"What did the man look like?"

"We couldn't see him very well from up there. He looked like an average man, that's all. He sat on the bench with Sacks and his back was to us. He was leaning toward Sacks. That's all I could see."

"Anything else? Anything at all?"

"He had a dog," Morgan said. "Yeah, he had a dog."

"What kind of a dog?" Jackson asked firmly, demandingly.

148

"Fuzzy," Markham said.

"What kind of fuzzy?"

"Furry. You know, the kind that looks like a small lion. Red and furry."

The three boys were animated, awake again, nervous, astounded.

"Red and furry," Jackson murmured. He pulled a walkie-talkie unit from his pocket and summoned aid.

"Red and furry," he repeated. "A chow? A chow?"

"Yeah," Morgan said, "that's it."

"Yeah," Samuels agreed.

"A chow," Jackson said, staring at Sacks' body.

A squad car came zooming down the mall from the south, turning the mall into a speedway. It stopped at the band shell and four men got out.

"Number four," Jackson told them, pointing to Sacks.

"Shit," one of them muttered.

"But these kids saw something," Jackson said to the other policemen.

Samuels, Morgan and Markham shuffled nervously.

"You three go home," Jackson said.

"I ain't walking through this park," Morgan said.

"Don't," Jackson said. He turned to the driver of the car. "Take these kids home, please. I don't want a fifth tonight."

He turned to the three boys. "Don't worry. Just be careful. We'll talk again soon. Be cool. I'm getting close now. Close. Take care of yourselves and I'll be around."

The three boys got into the squad car and it drove off. The three newly arrived policemen surrounded the body, checking it, taking notes. Jackson walked off alone toward the front of the band shell, leaned against the wall beneath the stage, and stared into the sky. His face was covered with sweat; he wiped it off with one hand and flicked his hand toward the ground.

As the others gently lifted the body, another car, then a second, arrived. Several policemen came running up from different directions. Jackson watched it all as if in a trance.

How many chows can there be in New York? he asked himself.

When Ronald Markham got home that night to the luxurious co-op apartment on the east side, he felt relieved to be there. The familiar velvet-covered living-room furniture, the satisfying chill of the air conditioning, even the sight of his mother propped up in bed watching the late movie on television comforted him. After the episode in the park he felt safe, although he thought that his heart was beating more rapidly than usual.

"I never see you in summer," his mother shouted. "Where were you today?" She was wearing a negligee, a costly one, and had her make-up on. It was not unusual, Ronald knew, for her to get up, get dressed and go out in response to those phone calls at three or four A.M.

He stared at her, considering her question. "In the park," he answered softly.

"What do you do there?"

"I hang out."

"You hang out?"

"With my friends."

"Well, it won't be long before school starts again. Better for you than hanging out in the park," she declared.

Ronald sat on the edge of the bed and thought that he loved her, but didn't really like her. He sensed the difference. They had little to do with each other most of the time; they led separate lives. He wasn't always certain that she would understand him if he told her something about what he had done.

He took the chance. "A kid I know was killed in the park tonight," he said calmly.

"What!" she shouted.

"Yeah," he said. "It's been happening. It's been in the papers. Four in a row now."

"You must not go to that park," she screamed. "You must not." She pounded the bed with her fist.

150

"The police want me to help."

"You? You?" she bellowed. "How dare they?"

"A policeman asked me and Samuels and Morgan to help."

"How? Are you supposed to carry a gun? Are you supposed to do that bastard's job for him? How?"

"Just by being alert, he said to us," Ronald said.

"Wonderful." She sighed. "Just wonderful."

The phone rang. Earlier than usual, Ronald thought.

"Yes?" she said into the phone softly. "Of course, of course. Absolutely. Just give me an hour. Certainly. I'll be downstairs. Mmmmmm. 'Bye."

She got out of bed and went into the bathroom. Ronald left her bedroom and fell onto his own bed, surrounded by the posters of rock stars he had nailed to the walls. He lit a cigarette and leaned back.

Almost an hour later his mother walked in, dressed. He thought that she looked beautiful, but he didn't say so.

"You've been smoking. Stop that. You know about cancer," she said. "And I don't want you to get into any trouble in the park. Do you understand me? Do you? Stay out of trouble."

He stared at her and wondered where she was going. Then he decided to say it. "When you go out at night like this, you know, what do you do?"

"What do you mean?" she asked firmly.

"Do you go to some guy's place and fuck?"

"It's none of your goddamned business," she screamed and stormed out of his room. He could hear her voice, repeating it: "It's none of your goddamned business," just before he heard the front door slam.

He lit another cigarette and thought about Samuels and Morgan and Jackson and the expression on Harvey Sacks's face after he died.

Jackson pushed his food around the plate with his fork and did not eat. "I blew it," he said to Mary. "I was so busy watching the three kids that I didn't pay attention to the fourth. Jesus Christ."

"Don't let it happen again," Mary said.

"Don't imitate the Captain. I've got enough problems." He poked at the food. "I'm sorry. You worked hard on this stuff and I can't eat it. I'm sorry."

"It's okay," Mary said. She got up and cleared the table. They went into the living room and sat on the sofa. He put his arm around her and talked.

"I was *there*. Close. I didn't think anything of it. A kid goes to get a drink of water. I'm staring at the shell and my three kids, and they seem to be up there, safe, and I relax. My God."

"So you don't have all that miraculous power, after all," Mary said.

"I never said I did. You're the one who seems to be fascinated by power. I have some power, yes, but I'm not using it very well these days."

"What are you supposed to do?"

"I'm supposed to find that guy, whoever he is, whatever he is, before he kills another kid. It's become a goddamned epidemic and I'm supposed to invent the vaccine. Right now. And inoculate every kid in the city within a few hours. And I don't know much. The guy has a dog. A chow. You don't see too many of those around the city. Not like poodles or cocker spaniels. We know that. But I can't find everyone who owns a chow and talk to each one and find out which one is a murderer. I haven't got the time. The guy could make his move again, at any minute. Where? When? I think I'm going crazy."

"Why?"

"The frustration. The damned tension that builds inside. The fist in my intestines. The headache that Excedrin hasn't named yet. The quivering feeling every time I see a guy walking his dog. The hollow feeling whenever I look at a kid. Especially when I look at Samuels or Morgan or Markham."

"Could they get hurt?"

"Could they get hurt? That's an understatement. They could

get wiped out. And if one of them goes, I go too. I can hang up that 'out to lunch' sign forever. The *Times* will call it 'gross negligence,' and the entire force will take a beating about how we abused the rights of minors and got one killed. Sometimes I wonder if I should have gotten them involved at all. It was so risky. But it seemed logical. They're *there*, in the park, every day. They seem to know how to take care of themselves. They better."

"And you better take care of them."

"I know, I know. I've got to be there *before* it happens. Simple, right? I've got to be there and the guy has to be there with the murder weapon and his goddamned dog and he's got to make a move and I've got to get to him first, when I know he's the right one. Without scaring him off. If he's there and doesn't make his move and doesn't have that gun with him I'm left hanging."

"How will you work it out?"

"I'm not sure yet. I'll keep an eye on the kids. If any one of them starts talking to a guy with a dog, I'll try to keep them in sight. The kids have to know to keep walking, not to stop or sit on the grass. I'll have to keep walking too. And pay attention. Not like last time. You know, it gives me the shakes."

"I believe you."

"I'll have some help, I suppose, but I can't count on them. Not because they're dumb or inept, but because I'm number one on this case."

"Does that make you nervous?"

"It makes me feel good and bad. Good that it's up to me, that it's my head against his, whoever he is. Bad that if I make a mistake someone I know gets killed."

Jackson was jittery, chain-smoking and drinking Coke after Coke.

"You won't get to sleep tonight," Mary said.

"Probably. But I'll try," he said.

"Let me know if you'd like to be helped toward exhaustion," she offered.

He smiled for the first time during their conversation.

Al Morgan puffed as he raced up the stairs to his mother's apartment. She had just gotten home from the restaurant and was sitting in a chair drinking a beer. The air conditioner in the living room was rattling, doing its best against the invading heat.

"Where you been?" she asked.

"Out all day," he said. He went to the kitchen and got a Coke out of the refrigerator, returned and sat down in the chair beside hers.

"You know, baby, there's been bad stuff going down in the park. I don't like you out there," she said.

"I know," he said. "Harvey Sacks got it tonight."

"Got what? And who's Harvey Sacks?" she asked. He could sense that her anger was rising.

"Got killed," he said, gently. "We were there. Samuels, Markham and me. We saw it. But we didn't see much. Sacks was talkin' to some dude and then the dude was gone and then the fuzz found Harvey and we saw that part of it."

"My God," she said. "You gonna get yourself killed too. You know that? You know what I'm saying? You hang out there and you gonna be wiped out like Harvey Sacks."

"Never happen," Al told her.

"My ass," she said. "I didn't bring you up, I didn't do all that shit, just to lose you in that damned park. You take care, you hear me?"

"I hear you," Al said.

"Don't you forget. I know what's happening. I read the papers. And there's been talk about all that in the restaurant. I know, baby, I know. I love you and I want you in one piece, like you are. I don't want to put your black ass in the ground. You hear me?"

"Yes, Momma. I hear you."

"You sure you do?"

"I'm sure," Al said. "But Jackson wants us to help."

"Help? Help? Who the hell is Jackson?"

154

"A cop. A black cop. He says he needs us to help."

"Well, isn't that a bucket of shit. He needs you? So it can be your ass gets chopped up and not his, I suppose. You tell that Jackson to put his own ass on the line, baby, and get yours out of it."

"I'm tired," Al said. He got up and headed toward his room. "I'm very tired."

She watched him in silence. When he went into his room, she got up and paced. Then she downed the rest of the beer and went into the kitchen for another. She looked out the window at Harlem. A few hookers were still strolling. A pusher she knew was getting out of his car; he was greeted by two needy junkies. Realizing she could not sleep, she went out, down the stairs and into her restaurant. She left her beer on a living-room table. When Al heard the door snap shut, he got out of bed, went into the living room and drank the beer she had left.

"I don't do this for strangers," Mary said, caressing Jackson's chest.

"Really?"

"Really. I let the others meditate about their problems. I work on yours."

"You do indeed," Jackson said, smiling broadly. "And how you do it!"

"Cost-free therapy. Salve for the soul. A spirit massage. With style, from good old Mary."

It was midnight and Jackson was weary. "Now I'm definitely tired," he said.

"No doubt. I do my work very well," she said.

"I helped. You didn't do it alone."

"True. And I congratulate you for your accomplishment."

"Thank you."

"Want some coffee?"

"Good idea."

Mary got out of bed and went into the kitchen. He could hear the dishes clatter, the coffee perk, Mary humming a Ray Charles tune.

He looked around the bedroom, at the furniture, at Mary's possessions, at the signs of her affluence. Money, he thought, money—and didn't pursue the thought. What was good about Mary? Her body, certainly, and how she used it, moving across a room or writhing in bed. She had good hands. Her success, coming up from the hell of Harlem and battling. He admired her spirit. But not her obsession to "make it," seemingly at any cost. He never had felt that way; he never had wanted to be famous, to be surrounded by fawning subordinates. He thought about his father, who played his instrument wondrously and never got rich. Did his father's eventual decay spring from that, from the absence of security? He really didn't know. They had talked, but they had not talked enough for him to understand. Perhaps, he thought, what I need is somewhere in between—neither the denial of money nor the insatiable wish to possess it.

Mary walked into the bedroom with two cups of coffee, put them on the night table and sat on the edge of the bed beside him.

"Tired?" she asked.

"Yes."

"Sleepy?"

"No."

"Want to talk?"

"About what?"

"About us?"

"No. Not now."

"Think we'll solve our problems?"

"Maybe. Maybe not," he said, and paused. "I don't mean to sound cold. I really don't."

"You know something? I don't know either. And I want to know."

"You'll know. And so will I. Later."

She got into bed beside him. They listened to the sound of the air conditioner, humming efficiently, and the random noises on the street below.

He leaned forward, as if in pain, said, "Shit," and fell back. His head hit the headboard. It hurt.

John Samuels didn't go to his west side home; he knew that his mother would be waiting up for him. He called her from a public phone booth and told her that he was fine and would be home soon, after visiting his father. He didn't mention what had happened in the park; he would talk to her about that later, when they were face to face and he could calm her down if she got nervous and anxious. He went to his father's. It was late, but he knew that his father wouldn't complain. He opened the door, which caught on the chain, making a loud noise.

"Who is it?" his father shouted. John could hear the television set in the background.

"Me. Who else?" John said through the narrow opening.

"Oh," his father said, coming to the door.

"Thought I'd pop in," John said.

"Fine," his father said. "Any time. The way my life is going, it's impossible for you to interrupt *anything.*" They both laughed.

"Want a Dr. Pepper? I'm just watching a good old movie. I've seen it before," his father said, turning off the set.

"Yeah. I'd like a cool drink," John said. His father went to the kitchen and got him one.

The apartment was cool and John was grateful for it. He reeked of sweat from his day outdoors and he was glad to be out of that. "I feel gross," he said.

"Been in the park today?" his father asked.

"Yeah."

"You know what's going on there these days?"

"You mean the murders? I know."

"You're as tall as I am and probably stronger, but you can appreciate the fact that I don't want you killed."

"I can appreciate that fact."

"Okay. I won't make a speech. I know it's summer and I know there isn't much for you to do. You should have gotten a job. But I don't want you to get hurt."

"There weren't any jobs. I tried. And I don't want to get hurt, either."

"Good. Then don't."

"One of the cops on the case, a black guy named Jackson, wants us to help. Me and Markham and Morgan. He says we won't get hurt, but he needs us."

"You're putting me on," his father said.

"No, I'm not. We know the park and we're there a lot and he figures we can help him."

"He's out of his tree. Or is it his gourd? Whatever. He has no right to ask that of you kids."

"I suppose."

"Doesn't the idea turn you off? I mean, do you really want to try to catch the killer? Really? Who says you have to qualify to be a hero? Who has that right?"

"I don't know, Dad. I don't know," John said. "To tell you the truth, the idea scares me. Tonight the three of us were at the band shell and we saw a kid we knew get killed. But we didn't see too much."

"Tell me about it," his father said, leaning forward in his chair.

"We were on top of the band shell, sitting up there just looking around. A kid we knew, Harvey Sacks, was up there with us and he got thirsty and went down and we saw him talking to some guy with a dog and when we went down he was dead. That cop, Jackson, got there, but too late. Another one-shot job, like the others."

"I don't believe it. I mean I *do,* but I don't want to," his father said.

"It *is* scary," John said.

"What am I supposed to say? Am I supposed to tell you to stay out of the park until they solve it? Am I supposed to bribe you to stay out of there? Am I supposed to send you on a vacation, out of this insane city?"

"No," John said. "Maybe there's nothing you have to say. Maybe I have to take care of myself."

"Fine. Take care of yourself. You decide what that means. I'll trust you. But if I'm wrong, or if anything terrible happens, I'll hate myself. Can you understand that?"

"Yes." John finished the Dr. Pepper. "I better go home," he said.

His father put his arm around his shoulder and led him to the door. "You take care," he said to John.

"I will."

After John had left, his father went to the phone and called his ex-wife.

"Sorry to call at this hour," he said into the phone. "Really, I am. But John just dropped in on his way to your place. He'll be home in a few minutes. Don't lean on him, please, even if he is beyond curfew. Why? Because one of his friends was killed in the park tonight. Yes. That's what I said. Don't be hysterical. Just listen, please.

"You know about those murders? Three kids, now four. Crazy. Abominable. Unbelievable. Talk to John about it. Maybe not when he gets home, maybe tomorrow. Do what you think is best. He does live with you. But urge him to be careful. There's some insane thing about the police wanting John and his friends to help. Help. Can you believe that? I don't think he really understands it all. He likes the idea of being heroic, but he must be scared to death as well. Sure. Do what you can. Christ, I wish the summer were over so he could be back in school and out of that park. Damned place. Fine. Talk to him. Listen, I'm sorry to call at this hour. Tell your husband that. But I thought it was important. Certainly. All right. I'll talk to you soon."

He put down the phone and stared into space. He saw his son often; although he didn't live with him, he did spend two or three nights a week with him. He enjoyed John's company, not simply

159

because John was his son. There was something strong about John that he admired, and John had a sense of humor that matched his own. When they were together, they laughed at each other without the slightest bitter edge to the laughter. The divorce was now eight years old, and he seemed to have grown closer to John through it all. He wanted that to continue. He didn't want to have to worry about John's safety.

He opened a Coke and began to sip it. As he did, he noticed that his hand was trembling. He took a Valium and went to bed.

As he made his way through a typical day of seeing patients, Dr. Weinstein had felt distracted. He didn't know why. It was Monday, much too early for him to be impatient for the week to end. On the other hand, he did not look forward to this weekend at the country house in Connecticut with his wife, who had been oddly hostile for several weeks. It might have been that he was bored by Mrs. Gilligan, who had just left his office after chanting her neurotic litany for an hour; he could not remember exactly what she had said during today's session. She would repeat it next week, fortunately, and he would try to be more attentive then.

Wilton arrived and Dr. Weinstein attempted to revive his interest. It was late in the afternoon; Wilton was the last patient today. He thought of that "cold slap in the face" from an idiotic television commercial he'd seen, and he greeted Wilton with a smile.

Wilton did not return the smile. He seemed distraught, and Weinstein studied him while both sat in silence.

"I am not well. Not well at all," Wilton said, almost in a whisper.

"What is it?" Weinstein asked.

"I don't know. You would call it 'free-floating anxiety.' I don't know what it is."

"I would call it free-floating anxiety?"

"Yes. That is how you speak."

"I do?"

"Yes."

They sat facing each other across Weinstein's desk in silence. Outside an ambulance, its siren shrieking, raced by. Children at play screamed at each other. A dog barked. A motorcycle in need of a new muffler roared aggressively.

"I am in pain," Wilton said, grimacing.

"What kind of pain?"

"Every kind known to man and science." Wilton sighed.

"Describe it."

"My body aches. My head aches. My psyche aches."

"Have you had a check-up lately?"

"No."

"Why not? You know better."

"I can't bear all the prodding and poking and the dull comments my internist feels obliged to make."

"That's a reason?"

"Perhaps not. Perhaps I don't have a reason."

"I see."

"My control is slipping away," Wilton said.

"Your control?"

"Yes, my ability to take charge of my own life."

"How is it happening?"

"I seem to sweat more than ever."

"It is summer. We all sweat."

"I am talking to someone and I realize that I am sweating profusely and my head begins to throb and I cannot concentrate."

"In the gallery?"

"Somewhat. I try to listen to the fools who buy from me, but I don't always remember what they say."

"And away from the gallery?"

"At home I seem to be all right. Bernard is my companion there."

"The dog."

"Yes."

"And when you're not at home or at the gallery?"

"I take long walks, in the park, with Bernard."

"In this heat? Why bother?"

"I walk. Through the park. Along the mall. I walk."

"And when you do, how do you feel?"

"Dreadful. It is that loneliness again, I suppose. We've talked about that."

"Yes."

"It isn't getting any better. I cannot seem to make friends. At least not easily. I try, you understand. God, I try. But there is something about me. Something. I can't seem to get anyone to be friendly. It is as if I am dying and those I approach know it and do not want to be present when I die."

"But you're not dying."

"It is a matter of definition."

"Who do you approach? How does one make friends in this city?"

"When I am walking with Bernard, I sit on a bench beside a young man and I talk to him. I have done that. They see me as a sort of leper. They do not respond at all, or if they respond what they have to say is inane, certainly not the basis for starting a friendship."

"You do not look like a leper to me," Weinstein said.

"That's kind of you," Wilton replied, staring blankly at the bookcase behind Weinstein.

"I'm not trying to be kind. I'm trying to be accurate."

"A policeman came to the gallery."

"A policeman? To buy a painting?"

"No."

"For what?"

"To show me a picture."

"What do you mean?"

"They were going from shop to shop. A boy had been murdered in the park and they were asking if anyone knew him."

"Yes, they do that in movies, as I recall."

"He showed me the picture and I didn't recognize the boy."

"I see."

"But later, much later, I did."

"You did recognize the boy?"

"Yes."

"You knew him?"

"No."

"But you recognized him?"

"Yes."

"How?"

"Perhaps I read the story in the paper, about his death. Perhaps I had known him once."

"Which?"

"I can't be sure."

"Is it important?"

"Very."

"Why?"

"Because if I had known him, it is possible that I killed him."

Weinstein looked at Wilton, whose neck muscles were conspicuously taut as he seemed to be leaning forward without actually moving his body.

"It is possible that you killed him?" Weinstein asked, sliding his chair against his desk and stretching his arms in front of him.

"Yes."

"It is possible that you killed him?" Weinstein repeated.

"Yes."

"Edmund, for God's sake, do you realize what you are saying to me? Do you realize what you're asking me to believe? Do you realize how long we've known each other?"

"Yes, to all those questions."

"And you are telling me that a boy was murdered in the park and you are the murderer. Edmund Wilton, gallery owner, independently wealthy, intelligent, in seemingly good health, is a murderer?"

"It is possible."

"How is it possible?"

"There have been other murders in the park this summer."

"There have?"

"Yes. All boys. I am not absolutely certain, you understand, but it is possible that I killed them all."

Weinstein could feel the edge of his desk pressed against his stomach. He pressed his hands on the top of the desk, spreading the fingers as wide as he could until he felt the pain of it.

"How? How did you kill them?" Weinstein asked calmly.

"With the gun I bought. Remember? Yes, with that gun."

"I remember it. Do you carry it with you when you take those walks."

"Yes, I do. I have."

"Do you have it with you now?"

"No. Only when I walk in the park."

"And if you have done all this, why would you do it? Why *you?* Why *it?*"

"Perhaps I am going crazy?"

"What does 'crazy' mean?"

"Out of control. My control, as I told you, seems to be slipping away."

"It is difficult for me to believe that my patient, Edmund Wilton, runs through the park looking for victims."

"I do not. Do not be a fool. I try to create conversation with such boys. They do not appreciate me."

"There is an age difference. Teen-age boys do not easily fall into conversation with older men. They have their own interests and their own language. It would be tough to sustain such a dialogue under the best of circumstances."

"No doubt," Wilton said. His eyes moved in short, sudden movements from ceiling to floor and back again.

"Do you understand that it is almost impossible for me to believe that you have done what you say you have done?"

"Yes, I can understand that. I am not certain that I believe it all myself."

164

Weinstein sat silently, staring at Wilton.

"Ah." Wilton emitted a long soft sigh. "You know, Doctor, I don't mean to sound melodramatic, but I am overwhelmed by sadness. For months I wondered why. I don't wonder now."

"What do you mean?"

"I have been looking for a friend. Infantile, isn't it? Childlike. Where have I looked? Among children. The innocents. When I was a child I was happy. I think at times that I haven't been happy since then. I have made money and I live comfortably and it is all insufficient. I have talked and talked to you about all that, but I never realized what I was doing. I would walk in the park. The park. A place where children play. And I would strike up a conversation with a young boy, but he would not really participate. There were moments when one of them would reject me, when I would seem to be in a trance. I had never felt that way before. I needed a companion, like some old man who fears loneliness and pleads for friendship, or tries to demand it. I didn't know how to get it. I tried and I tried and I tried. Either I didn't know how or it was impossible. Impossible, always. I have, with the very best intentions, turned my life into a tragedy. I have not been in control. I do not know if I am responsible anymore. My past, my childhood—bits of it—and my present seem to be superimposed. I do not know anything."

"Would you like to check into a hospital, a comfortable one, for a few days? To rest. To feel better. To talk about all this at greater length."

"Not yet."

"Why don't I give you a prescription for something that will enable you to relax?"

"It won't be necessary," Wilton said, getting up. "Funny, but I often know when it is time to leave, without even glancing at my watch. It is that time now."

"There is no need to run, Edmund. If you want to talk about this now, we can talk about it. I don't have any other patients coming in after you today. We can talk."

165

"Another time," Wilton said. He placed a folded piece of news-paper on Weinstein's desk, waved his hand and walked out of the office.

Weinstein folded the paper again and again, until it was small enough to fit into the palm of his hand. He folded it and unfolded it while he thought about Wilton. He got up from behind his desk and walked over to the window. He looked out at the street, at the cars passing by, the mothers walking their children, the teen-agers on bicycles, the trucks, the trees and the sun.

Slowly he unfolded the paper. It was a page from the *Times* containing a story about teen-age boys murdered in Central Park. Weinstein read it carefully, line by line, comparing the story to what Wilton had said to him.

Had Wilton, in some sudden psychotic shift, assumed the guilt for these crimes? Weinstein wondered. Or had he suddenly be-come another person, someone Weinstein did not really know, someone Weinstein had not been able to treat?

Weinstein was distracted momentarily with the thought of his wife. He snapped out of that and paced. Now this week would have to be a shambles, he thought, whatever happened. There was not a single way he could salvage some peace from it. He would not go home. He could not. He phoned his wife and told her he would stay in his office; he had done that before. What should he do? He sat down and tried to concentrate. His mind raced down corridors offering alternative means of action. He was not certain what would be the best move for him to make. He could continue to explore Wilton's "confession," he thought, but that would take time. Assuming it was not a part of reality, he might lead Wilton to understand it, to agree to be treated more intensively. That was a serious matter. In fact, Wilton had become a serious matter. Weinstein could not make a judgment easily.

He left the office and walked.

He felt exhausted, and as he walked he felt the exhaustion grow. He felt weak. He stopped in a small restaurant and ate a hamburger without enthusiasm. He drank three cups of coffee, paid the bill and left. He resumed his walk, without destination.

He stopped in a bar and ordered a beer. He did not drink often, but he was tired and had to sit. He sipped the beer and thought about Wilton. His own guilt expanded as he considered their relationship. He had been listening to the man for months and had missed something important. If Wilton had been accurate about the murders. Perhaps he should get out of private practice and into research? The thought didn't contribute to his understanding of Wilton, so he abandoned it.

If Wilton did kill those boys, he did so while in a psychotic state resembling temporary amnesia, he thought. He is not a killer. Frustrated, angry, rejected. All of those, but not, Weinstein thought, an obvious murderer. Yet he could have done it. He could have killed. What does that say about me? he thought. He was cooler, thanks to the air conditioning in the bar and the chilled beer, but he was still exhausted, debilitated.

He paid for the beer and walked out into the hot night. It was nine P.M. on Monday. Several hours had vanished while he had walked and eaten and sipped the beer. He walked back to his office, feeling both weak and agitated simultaneously.

He sat behind his desk fidgeting, making notes on his pad. He turned on the radio and listened to some classical music. He could not concentrate. He dialed Wilton's number. No answer. He is not at home, Weinstein said to himself.

At eleven P.M. he took a ten-milligram Valium and stretched out on the couch. I use it more than my patients do, he thought; they prefer the chair. He smiled weakly and fell asleep.

He awoke at 5 A.M., still tense. He returned to his desk, picked up the phone and dialed 911.

When a voice sounded on the other end, he said, "What I am about to say to you may or may not be useful. I am a psychiatrist."

Tuesday

Jackson drew circles lightly with his finger on Mary's exposed hip. The skin was smooth, a flawless texture. He turned his head slowly, still groggy, and looked at the clock. Three A.M. Mary did not move; she breathed steadily. He leaned back against the headboard and stared out the window.

He thought about the crimes, ploddingly, as if going through a series of dull yellowing files.

He listed his conclusions. The murder weapon had been the same in every case; Ballistics had returned its reliable verdict. Someone owned a .22-caliber pistol and was using it. No one had reported any accompanying sound; there was a silencer attached to the weapon.

The man—and it was a man he was looking for, not a woman or a boy or a young girl—owned a dog. A chow. He walked that dog in Central Park. He was neatly dressed, not a conspicuously sloppy person whose appearance might call attention to him.

He was not, Jackson was convinced, one of the park's crazies, or one of the city's conspicuous lunatics, the kind he could spot a block away. The ones who wore long overcoats in summer. The ones who babbled on buses and subways. The ones who *looked* crazy. He was another sort.

He did not kill when there were crowds around. If he wanted

to be caught, in that odd psychopathic way that some criminals do, he did not want to be mobbed by his captors. He killed in a public place, of course, but he exercised some care.

He spent much of his time in the park in the area near the band shell, along the mall. Jackson assumed that he lived nearby, that the park would be a natural place for him to go. He guessed that the man lived not far from the park, that he had been walking his dog in the park before any of these crimes were committed.

An obsessive, he concluded. This man always got close to the victim, very close, put the barrel of the gun against the boy's heart and fired once. Perfection. Fastidious. Obsessive. Most murderers will settle for a sloppy death; this one will not. And he would have to involve the boy, somehow, to get that close, to make it work. So he could not be a visible maniac who might scare off the victim before he became a victim. Personable, perhaps, or simply tolerable.

It is possible, Jackson felt, if he were indeed psychotic, detached from reality, or in and out of it, that he would not necessarily realize what he was doing, or that anyone might be looking for him. He had seen cases like that before. It was a hunch, no more, but he stressed it more and more in his thoughts.

His theories were based largely on hunches, he thought. There weren't enough clues in this case and it was maddening. This killer, by intention or style, was not easily categorized. And with so little evidence, it might turn out to be a matter of waiting, of being patient and ready. Clever crimes could be solved cleverly, he thought, but some crimes required only diligence, effort, perseverance. He remembered a lieutenant saying to him at the police academy, "Sometimes you just wait. You can't do anything else. If you're *there*, you solve it. If you're not, somebody dies."

Mary sighed "Yes" in her sleep and wiggled.

Jackson thought about the three boys—Samuels, Morgan and Markham. He didn't like the idea of "using" them as decoys. A decoy can become a corpse, and if anything happened he would be in trouble. He weighed the alternatives and discounted them.

Members of the force could not pose as teen-agers. He needed the real thing. If he staked out as many men as the force could spare, in various disguises, he should be able to protect the boys. If the stakeouts were as vigilant as he hoped they'd be. How could he be certain that one of the boys would be chosen? He couldn't, but he wanted to risk the bet. Boys were the victims, and he had three of them on his side. He had strayed too far when Sacks had been killed; that wouldn't happen again. He'd get more help as well.

He had been pushing hard on this case, fruitlessly, and the expenditure of energy, coupled with the frustration, was beginning to turn to rage. He had to crack it this weekend, somehow, but he couldn't do it alone. He would need the killer's cooperation. He hoped he would get it.

He resumed drawing circles on Mary's hip.

Wilton had gone to the park from Weinstein's office. It was late when he returned home. He slept fitfully and awoke Tuesday morning at four, shaken by the identical nightmare he had experienced the night before his last visit to his doctor. In it, he was in the park, surrounded by young people. They were friendly and allowed him to dominate, in a cheerful way, their conversation. Several of the faces were familiar, all boys. Suddenly the entire group walked away from him. He screamed at them, took out the gun and fired once. They ran. The gun became hot, like melting, flaming metal, and he dropped it. And awoke, dizzy and covered with sweat.

Bernard was asleep at the foot of the bed. He sat up, leaned forward and stroked the dog's head gently. The dog looked up at him, yawned, fell back into sleep.

He got up slowly and went to the kitchen. He made a cup of espresso and sat drinking it, staring out the window. He glared at the darkness. Only one light was visible, someone awake in a neighboring building. The light went out and he returned to his coffee.

173

The dream and the reality coursed through his head. He rarely remembered his dreams; this was one he could not forget. It stayed with him in precise detail. The faces appeared as vividly to him now as they had in the dream. He had not mentioned the dream to Weinstein; he had spoken of the reality. Or rather the conclusion he had reached about the reality, piecing it together carefully from both his dream and the far reaches of his memory. It had not been accessible at first; he was forced to struggle toward it, almost against his will. But he had struggled, sorted, concluded. The realization had magnified his continuing depression. He was, he knew, moving in and out of a sense of reality. He did not want to believe it, yet it had to be true.

He wept, for them and for himself. The tears dropped onto the front of his silk pajamas. He wiped his face with a clean handkerchief, dabbed at his eyes. He sat in front of the table without realizing that time had passed until he sipped the coffee and it was cold. He got up, washed the cup and saucer, put them in the rack to dry.

He walked back into his bedroom. Bernard was still asleep. He petted him again. He turned off the light and tried to go back to sleep but couldn't. He could see the day arriving through the bedroom window, the beginning of light. He got out of bed again, shaved, took a bath, got dressed and went into the living room.

He removed all the soldiers in his collection, one by one, from the cabinet and sat on the floor with them. He arranged them in perfect rows and studied them admiringly. I should go somewhere, he thought. Not far, not a trip, not to London or Paris, but somewhere. *Out.* He felt the weight of the cumulative depression and an edge of terror, but he could not define it well enough to act upon it.

I must go out, he thought: I must walk. What day is it? Tuesday. The gallery. He would go there.

It was five-thirty A.M. and Jackson didn't know if he should get up and make himself a cup of coffee or stay in bed, to avoid awakening Mary. He stayed in bed and stared at Mary's face.

She needed a hero, he thought, and he was not really a hero. He solved problems. In an almost intellectual way—and he did not think of himself as an intellectual—he could be given the facts, the findings, and reach logical conclusions. He did that better than most of the policemen he knew, and that ultimately would be the source of his reward. He was not certain that promotions would be enough for him or if they would be irrelevant. What he needed, he thought, was the consistent sense of challenge and the idea that what he was doing was helping others.

Mary wanted a man in expensive clothes, a guy who drove a Mercedes, who inspired smiles of recognition from headwaiters and timidity from those who worked for him. She wanted influence; she was after it herself, but if she could combine hers with a man's it would be the satisfying combination.

He felt a bit sad about the realization. They had had some good times together. And some bad. But more good than bad. Was that the criterion? More good than bad. Fifty-one per cent? It didn't seem to be enough. Could she change? Could he? Could he depend on either? He didn't know. He felt restless, edgy, tense.

The phone rang.

Mary reached for it, picked it up and listened. Then she turned toward Jackson and handed him the phone. "Goldman," she said sleepily.

"Mark?" Jackson said softly. "Jesus, Mark, it's five-thirty in the morning."

Goldman apologized, then said, "Warren, get yourself out of bed. We've got something."

"What?" Jackson wanted to know.

"We got a call this morning. A Doctor Weinstein, a psychiatrist. Said he has a patient, described the guy—middle-aged upper-class kind of guy, owns a dog. Said the guy was in to see him yesterday, usual session, and was talking about killing kids. The doctor didn't much like telling it to us, but he said he felt he had to, even if it wasn't the right thing for him to do, even if his patient was making it up. He didn't even know about the murder last night."

"Go on," Jackson said, sitting up stiffly.

"Said something about pedophilia. Know what it is?"

"No."

"Something to do with a weird compulsion to be with kids when you're an adult. Not your normal kind of thing."

"What else?"

"Said he couldn't be sure about all this or about anything else for that matter. Almost seemed to be putting himself down. But he said he couldn't let his doubts hang over his head, so he called us. He said if it's true the man could be desperate. And he can't find him. He wants to be notified immediately if we find him, whether he's trying it again or not. Even if he's not the guy we want."

"You've got his name and phone number? And his patient's name and address?"

"Of course."

"Give them to me."

Goldman dictated and Jackson wrote it down on a pad that Mary handed him.

"Okay," Jackson said. "Okay. I'll be down there. Tell the Captain and Fahey and the others, if you haven't already. You did? Good. I'll be there and we'll all talk. Don't do anything until I get there. I'm on my way."

He put down the phone and got out of bed.

"Want some coffee?" Mary asked.

"No. Looks like it could be a very busy day, not to mention the night." He got dressed quickly. Mary remained in bed.

He stood in the doorway. "I'll let myself out," he said. "Don't get up."

"Will you call me and tell me what happened?" she asked.

He didn't reply.

"Will you?"

He shrugged.

"Will you call me?"

"I don't know," he said. "One problem at a time."

She waved at him and he left.

She waited a moment, then got out of bed. Her body gleamed in the shafts of sunlight piercing the room. She went to the window and saw Jackson running toward a vacant cab.

He's in good shape, she thought, and without quite knowing why, she felt like crying.

He got Bernard and left the apartment. The night doorman was still on duty, half-asleep, oblivious of the man and the dog leaving the building at the early hour. Bernard seemed lethargic. He did not tug at the leash; he walked slowly beside his master.

They made their way through the heavy early morning air to the gallery. He unlocked the door, entered, locked the door behind him. He went to his office at the rear of the gallery and sat down beside his desk. Bernard curled up in a large leather chair.

He looked at his account book. He had not sold a work in a month. He seemed mildly surprised by the recognition, but simply closed the book and put it back into the drawer. He stared at the Picasso lithograph on the wall, thinking again that it had been too good to sell; he was glad that he had kept it for his own pleasure.

The leather bag was on the desk. He snapped it open; the gun was inside. He closed it, whipped the strap over his shoulder, seized Bernard's leash and left the gallery.

He walked down Madison Avenue. There were more people on the street now. The day had arrived and with it those people who greeted it avidly. He did not. He thought about his distaste for the early morning, despite all the seductive pastoral poems he had read about sunrise and early morning dew and the scents of nature.

He stopped at Schrafft's for breakfast, eating the scrambled eggs and giving the ham to Bernard, who sat obediently beside his chair. They were the first customers of the day and the waitress paid more attention than he liked. He responded curtly to her and she left to hover elsewhere. He finished and looked at the check. How much is 15 per cent of $2.25? he thought, concentrating. He reached into his pocket and left thirty-five cents on the table. He paid the check and resumed his walk.

He passed other art galleries. He knew most of them and disliked most of their owners, whom he saw as an elitist, condescending lot. No doubt, he thought, they saw him as a recluse in their midst. I do not care, he said to himself; I do not care. He had repeated that chant to himself before, whenever he thought about his competition.

Years ago a customer had come into his gallery to tell him in the course of her browsing that Rosenson, then the "popular" gallery owner, had told her not "to bother" looking at "those pathetic remnants" in his gallery. "I sell them and I do not defraud anyone," he had said to her. She did not buy anything.

He kept walking, as if he could not stop. He went down Madison to 59th, then over to Fifth. Bernard seemed to come to life when the park came into view; his sluggishness vanished and he began to tug at the leash. They entered the long path toward the zoo, walking between the rows of benches. An old woman with a shopping bag in her lap sat serenely, drooling. He noticed her momentarily, then snapped his head away in disgust. Several mothers chattered in French while their infants slept in their carriages. A British nanny sat clutching the bar of a large and elegant carriage while the child within it cried relentlessly. The nanny, unmoved, tapped at the bar, rocking the carriage slightly, and stared ahead.

It was now late in the morning and the park was beginning to fill up, as it did on weekdays in summer. He saw a Frisbee sail through the air and followed its arc to the outstretched hand of an eager boy. He stopped, looked at the boy, then moved on, with Bernard now excitedly ahead of him, the leash taut.

He stopped at the zoo. Small children were waving at the seals, barking at the lions and tigers, laughing at the monkeys. He walked past it all, heading north.

A pretzel vendor distracted him. He had not eaten a pretzel in years. He did not know why he felt the particular craving now, but he paused and bought one. It was thick and cottony and salty and he enjoyed it. He thought of it as an early lunch; he did not have an appetite for more than that today.

North of the zoo, he wound his way along the path, past more benches, more mothers, more children. The park was growing noisier too; that was something he noticed as the day progressed. Dogs racing and barking. Toddlers making their little sounds, nonsense syllables and giggles. Older boys shouting, as if they did not know how to speak softly. The sound of a ball against a glove. Foreign languages, from the familiar rattle of city Spanish to the exotic chewing sound of Russian and the harsh assertiveness of German.

His depression persisted. Again he felt lonely despite the sounds and the crowds and the conspicuous expressions of summer joy. He saw a teen-age boy sitting on a bench and started to veer toward him to initiate a conversation, but the boy got up suddenly, without looking at him, and bolted off. He resumed his walk resolutely.

"He isn't at his apartment," Fahey said.

"And he isn't at the gallery," Goldman added.

"So where the hell is he?" Fahey asked.

"I don't know," Jackson said. "Tell me again what the shrink said."

"He said that he had this patient, a guy he'd been seeing for months and there didn't seem to be anything terribly wrong with

179

the guy except that he was depressed and said he was lonely," Fahey said.

" 'There didn't seem to be anything terribly wrong,' " Jackson said. "Kiss my ass."

"He said that he wondered about calling us. You know, he thought maybe the guy was being perverse or testing his reaction or something and maybe he just read about it in the papers and was feeding it back. Then he figured he might as well call, just in case, although he did say he had his doubts. Covered himself, you might say."

"You might," Jackson said. "He didn't call us fast enough."

"We didn't move as fast as we might have," Goldman said. "But then what if we did? Unless we found the gun, what good would it have done?"

"Maybe it would have saved another life," Jackson grunted.

"Don't get righteous," Fahey snapped. "Go find him."

"Sure. Go find him."

"We know he's not at home, right? We know he's not at his gallery. We know that much," Goldman said.

"Terrific," Jackson said. "Just terrific."

"Maybe he left town," Fahey suggested.

"Doubt it. I just doubt it."

"You're feeling nasty because I had to call you at Mary's and get you out of that lovely sack," Goldman said.

"That's part of it. But not much of it."

"Enough of this shit," Fahey shouted. "Enough. Get your ass into the park, along with all the others we've got out there. We haven't had time to spread a description, but *you* know who we're looking for, so go out there and look."

"Where?"

"In the park. Where else?"

"Yes. In the park. Do you know what's going on in the park today? Four hundred people are getting laid. Several hundred others are getting high. More than that are just hanging out. Go find him. Sure. I'll go find him."

180

"And there's a concert set for the band shell tonight," Goldman added. "Just thought I'd keep you up to date."

"Wonderful. All I have to do is get up on the stage, sing, and scan the audience until I find him. Easy."

"If you don't find him before that," Fahey said. "And anyway, what the fuck is supposed to be easy for us?"

"Nothing," Jackson said.

"Do you know all of our men? Who they are?"

"Yes," Jackson said. "There'll be no confusion."

"Okay. Then get out there and hustle your ass."

The meeting broke up and Jackson went to a public phone and called Samuels. It was eleven A.M. Samuels was sleepy. Yes, he could get Morgan and Markham and meet Jackson at noon in front of the book stalls on Fifth Avenue at 60th. Yes, he would. No, he would not go back to sleep.

At noon they were all there.

"We think we know something," Jackson told the boys. "We think we may know who we're looking for. It is not the kind of exact answer we wanted, but there are some coincidences at least that are encouraging. And we can't find the guy. He's not at home or at the gallery he owns. So we're hoping he's out there." Jackson pointed toward the park.

"So are thousands of others," Markham said.

"Indeed, my man. Indeed," Jackson said.

"So?" Markham asked.

"So? So we'll do our best, pay attention and pray to God that we get lucky."

"Makes me very nervous," Samuels said.

"Scares the shit out of me," Morgan added.

"You want to know something?" Jackson asked. "Scares me too. But believe me, I'll be *there*, somewhere. Not like last time. I won't be far away this time. I'll be there. With my friends. Trust me about that."

"Okay, okay. You'll be there. It takes the guy a second to pull the trigger. You can't move that fast. And how do we know that he'll want to rap with one of us? He's got thousands to choose from," Samuels said.

"We don't know. It's roulette. But you three are the right age and size and type. Maybe we'll get lucky."

"It depends on what you mean by luck," Samuels said. "After today I may just tip. I may just forget about all of this." Markham and Morgan nodded in agreement.

"Here's what we're going to do," Jackson said. "We're going to hang out on the mall, up and down, near the shell. Just hang out, separately. Not the three of you together. One here. One there. One somewhere else. Hang out."

Samuels shook his head slowly. Morgan and Markham just stared at Jackson.

"If nothing happens this afternoon, fine. Eat a hot dog." He handed each boy two dollars for dinner. "Tonight there's a band concert. Move around. Sit on a bench. When it's over, stay there for an hour. If nothing happens by then, you can leave, go home, be out of all this. I'll worry about it myself after that. Fair?"

"Almost," Samuels said. "But the longer this goes on, the more my stomach hurts. I'm not joking."

"I'm not either," Jackson said. "And listen to me. If any of you feel weird about this during the day, get out. Go home. I'm not forcing you to help. You do what feels best for you. Understand?"

"Yes," Samuels said, speaking for all three.

"Remember, we're looking for a middle-aged guy, dapper, sort of quiet type, with a chow dog. For today at least, if any other kind of guy wants to talk to you, move on, fast. We haven't got time to waste. Now, let's go. One at a time," Jackson instructed. "Samuels first. Then Morgan. Then Markham. Into the park, not too close, not too far apart."

"Where will you be?" Samuels asked.

"Behind all three."

"Don't get lost," Samuels said, forcing a smile.

"I'll do my best."

182

"One last question," Samuels said. "What do I do if he finds me?"

"Keep moving. Don't sit beside him. Keep him moving; keep him talking. Head for an open space. Head toward home. Don't panic."

"Man . . ." Samuels began. He did not finish the sentence.

The boys, one by one, walked into the park at the 60th Street entrance, past the benches lined with people, toward the zoo, toward the mall.

He realized that he was weary. Too much walking, he thought. Too little sleep. He took Bernard off the path to a grassy hillside. He took out a large handkerchief, spread it on the ground and sat on it; he tied Bernard's leash to a nearby tree. Bernard relaxed into a lazy nap. It was midafternoon now, but he was tired. He remembered that he had gotten up at four A.M. Not enough sleep, he thought. He remembered the dream again. He tried to dismiss it from his mind. He leaned back on the grass, thinking that the grass would stain his shirt. But he was unwilling to sit up any longer. He stretched out on the grass, the handkerchief's inadequacy visible beneath him.

He stared at the blue sky as if it were a backdrop for any images he might summon. He thought about his mother, how very much he missed her kindness, her attentiveness, her generosity. His life had changed, and not simply because of grief, when she died. When she lived they would have dinner once or twice a week and reminisce. They would joke and laugh and talk about how important they were to each other. Then she was gone, he thought, and any potential he might have had for vitality went with her.

He wanted to sleep, but he could not. The idea of sleeping in the park was foreign to him. He looked up at the sky and thought. When he glanced at his watch, he was surprised to see that it was six P.M. He hadn't noticed the sun move, the light change. He felt disoriented. He was hungry. He stood up, picked up the handkerchief and folded it carefully into a square. He dabbed his face with

183

it and put it into his pocket. He untied Bernard and walked north again, toward the mall.

He bought another pretzel and a Coke, smiling at the departure from one of his cherished habits, eating a reasonable dinner. At the end of the mall he could see the crowds and he remembered that there was a concert tonight. He had attended a few of them and had concluded that they were a pleasant enough way, an inoffensive way, to pass a few hours. A Sousa march or two to keep the blood flowing, to distract one from troubles.

He proceeded toward the band shell.

It was a debilitatingly hot night. There was not a breeze and the air was filled with thousands of gnats attacking the spectators in diving clusters. The Naumburg Symphony Orchestra was in the band shell, conductor Jacques Singer in front of it. Promptly at seven-thirty P.M. the concert began, to an audience that filled every bench and strayed in waves behind the seats.

After playing "The Star-Spangled Banner," the orchestra played Grieg's "Heart Wounds," Op. 34, Mozart's "Haffner" Symphony and Schumann's Concerto for Cello, Op. 129, in A minor, with Leslie Parnas as soloist. The audience was appreciative and restless at the same time, trapped in the heat and by the swarms of gnats.

At intermission few people moved. They slapped at their necks and arms and clothes, staining them with dead gnats. They stared into the cloudless sky at the gleaming moon; they chatted aimlessly, awaiting the second half of the concert.

Samuels made his way through the crowd, slapping at the back of his neck, his arms, his T-shirt, where dark blotches of dead gnats offended him. He had not seen Morgan or Markham since two P.M.; they were somewhere in the mass of people, he suspected, but he had not seen them. He had not seen Jackson either since their meeting earlier in the day. He shoved his way toward a soft-drink vendor and bought a cherry soda.

He leaned against a tree, facing the shell, and wondered what he was doing there. It was almost evening now. He felt a strong impulse to go home and watch television, to talk to his mother, to talk to her husband, to take a shower and wash his hair, to listen to records. He had concluded that his cooperation with Jackson had been a mistake, an attempt at heroism that was not consistent with his belief about staying alive at all costs. The cherry soda was lukewarm; it heightened his wish to go home, where the soda was always chilled and the environment always safe.

This music didn't delight him either. It was not his kind of music. He would rather be listening to Hot Tuna or the Grateful Dead or, of course, the Rolling Stones' new album that his father had bought for him. He thought about his father, briefly, and thought fondly of him.

He felt a hand on his shoulder and he turned. He saw the face first; he didn't recognize it. Then he saw the dog.

"Good evening," Wilton said. "Another hot one, certainly, but the music is good and free."

"Yes," Samuels said, thinking, My God, here he is. "Yes."

"Yes what?"

"Yes, it is good and free." Samuels forced a smile.

"Do you come here often?"

"Yes. Day and night," Samuels said.

"Perhaps I've seen you here before?" Wilton asked.

"It's possible."

"Yes."

Samuels stared at him. He is a respectable man, he thought. The dog barked and Samuels looked at it. A chow, he thought. He felt a twinge in his stomach.

"Would you like to walk along with us?" Wilton asked. "I'm taking Bernard for his usual evening stroll and it would be a pleasure to chat with you along the way."

"I'm here with some friends," Samuels said. His heart was pounding. "Maybe after the concert, if you're still around."

"Splendid," Wilton said. "I'll look for you."

"Do that," Samuels said. He spotted Morgan, near the edge of the stage, his round black face gleaming with perspiration. He ran to him.

"What's happenin'?" Morgan asked.

"He found me."

"Who found you? The—"

"Yes."

"Oh, man, I don't like this."

"I don't either. Just find Jackson and let him know. He wants me to come along while he walks his dog after the concert. He'll be looking for me after the concert. You be looking for me too, please."

Morgan didn't speak. He shook his head in disbelief and ran into the crowd.

Samuels walked back to behind the last row of seats. The orchestra returned to the stage, and he stood there and watched the musicians assemble. Singer returned, raised his baton, and the music resumed. Prokofiev's *Symphonie Classique;* Peter Mennin's Toccata from *Fantasia for Strings;* Tchaikovsky's Serenade in C Major, Op. 48.

Samuels' eyes searched the crowd, which had begun to diminish as the concert moved toward its conclusion. Where was Morgan? He couldn't see him. Where was Markham? Nowhere. Jackson? Not to be seen. Samuels felt both drained and terrified. He wanted to go home. The orchestra played its finale, "America," the audience applauded, the concert ended. Crowds moved in streams in all directions.

He looked around. No man. No chow. Enough, he thought. If I'm to do this, let him find me.

He began to walk. He was out of money and decided to walk across the park toward the west side and home. Once he got north of the shell, he followed a path heading north, then west. No one else seemed to be taking this route; they were probably getting out of the park more expeditiously.

He passed the boat pond and could see the statue of Hans

Christian Andersen next to it. On his left he saw the boat house, its parking lot. He hopped onto the park drive and kept walking. I missed him, he thought, or he missed me. Fine with me, he said to himself. Just fine. He kept walking.

At that moment he felt something brush against his leg. It was a light touch, and soft, like a gentle wisp of wind. He looked down and saw the chow.

His eyes went from the fluffy dog along its leash to the hand that held it. Then up to the face.

"You didn't look for me after the concert," Wilton said.

"I couldn't find you," Samuels said. He felt the twinge in his stomach again.

"No doubt, in that crowd," Wilton said.

"No doubt," Samuels said. He didn't know what to say.

"Well, walk along with us, as we planned. It's a fine evening for a stroll, don't you think?"

"Yes."

"The music had some charm, don't you think? But the heat was oppressive and the air was filled with those awful flying things."

"Gnats," Samuels said.

"Yes. That's what they are."

Where is Jackson? Samuels thought. He tried to look around, inconspicuously, but he didn't see anyone he knew. Where are Morgan and Markham? he thought. He considered running, just breaking away from Wilton and vanishing. Wilton could not catch him if he did that. He was afraid. At the same time he felt that he could trust Jackson. If Morgan found him. He felt terrified again, a fear that he had never felt before. I'll do it, I'll do it, he chanted to himself. I'll do what I promised I'd do. He decided he would not look at Wilton and he would walk with him toward the west side. If the guy did anything alarming, he would run.

Jesus Christ, he thought. My God, *where is Jackson?*

"I live alone in this city and I work largely alone," the man said, "so it is a pleasure to be able to chat with someone. I hope you don't mind."

187

"No," Samuels said, feeling the sweat coming through his T-shirt. He looked around for Jackson. No sign.

They continued to walk, passing the monument to King Jagiello of Poland.

"Good God!" the man said. "A monument to a Polish king. Only in Central Park."

Samuels wanted to laugh. It seemed like the natural thing to do, but he couldn't.

"Don't you think that's absurd, really absurd?" the man asked.

"I suppose it is," Samuels said. "Like all those Polish jokes."

"My name is Wilton, by the way," the man said. "Edmund Wilton."

"John Samuels," Samuels said, automatically extending his hand. They shook hands and kept walking.

"Sometimes when it is very hot out, I feel overwhelmed by the heat itself. And the noise. But then there are times when the noise seems to vanish."

"Weird," Samuels said.

"Not really. We do what we have to do."

Samuels wondered what that meant and said nothing while he thought about it. He hoped that Jackson was nearby, watching.

"You're not permitted to be silent," the man said, laughing softly.

"Sorry," Samuels said. "I was thinking."

"About what?"

"About you," Samuels said, astounded at his own assertiveness.

"Oh?"

They turned a corner and were on the Great Lawn, near the pond, with the Belvedere Castle outlined against the moonlight. The field seemed almost empty. Samuels looked around. A couple were making love beneath a tree. Another were hugging each other on a bench. On another bench an old woman slept, stretched out to consume the entire bench. He heard giggles from a clump of bushes, lascivious sounds in the night. Otherwise he could not see much.

They followed the sidewalk toward the pond; beyond it the sidewalk led to the west side. Samuels looked up and could see the tower of the Beresford on Central Park West at 81st Street. It was dark, despite the moonlight and the glittering lights on the west side, and Samuels didn't know what to say next.

Jackson's mouth was dry. There was a dull ache in the back of his neck, but he kept running. When Morgan had found him, the concert was almost over. He had watched Samuels and waited. Nothing. The concert ended and he saw Samuels head toward home. He had followed him, keeping out of sight, ducking from bush to bush, behind trees. On his walkie-talkie he had announced Samuels' movements to the others, checked on the location of stakeouts. Then he saw Wilton. He could almost hear his own heartbeat; he held his hand to his chest as if to muffle it. He watched Wilton and Samuels move along the road, onto the path forty yards ahead of him.

He wanted to rush up immediately. He thought about that quickly. He liked Samuels. But he needed that case in court; he needed that gun. He stayed at a distance.

Then he heard a thrashing sound in the bushes beside him and instinctively he turned. The sound stopped, then came out of the bushes again. Jackson separated the branches rapidly and stepped forward; two stray dogs were wrestling. He leaped out and ran back onto the path. Wilton and Samuels were out of sight. My God, he thought. No, not again. He removed his service revolver from the shoulder holster under his shirt and began to run as fast as he could into the darkness ahead, toward the Great Lawn.

Wilton spoke. "My life is wretched," he groaned, surprising Samuels. Samuels looked at him carefully for the first time. He was well dressed, neat, the sort of man Samuels wouldn't normally be meeting or walking through the park with. But his face seemed twisted, distorted, in pain.

"You okay?" Samuels asked, wondering why he was asking.

"No. No. I am alone. And yet I have done horrible things. Horrible things."

"What?" Samuels asked.

"Does it matter? The torment is mine. You cannot help me."

"Probably," Samuels said. He touched Wilton gently on the shoulder. Wilton stared at him numbly.

"Let's sit beside the pond."

"I should get home," Samuels said.

"For a moment," Wilton said.

They walked toward the edge of the water. Wilton sat down, releasing his grip on Bernard's leash. The dog sat down beside him. Samuels continued to stand.

"Sit," Wilton said.

"I'd rather stand," Samuels said.

"All right. You know, I am not really an old man, yet I feel very old. There are older men who do not feel as old as I do. I do not understand it."

Thoughts raced in conflict through Samuels' mind: This man does not seem like a psycho. This man has killed four boys. This man seems sad. This man is dangerous.

"You know . . . what did you say your name was?"

"Samuels. John."

"You know, John, I have lived my life respectably. Until a few months ago I did no harm to anyone. I don't know what has happened. Or at least I didn't know for weeks. Then I knew. I had a grotesque dream that told me what I had to know, about what I had done with my life, about what I had done with the lives of others. I knew."

Samuels did not know what to say, so he said nothing. His eyes darted around the field, across the pond, toward the castle, toward the buildings on the west side. Nothing seemed to be moving.

"I don't know what to say," Samuels said.

"That's perfectly all right," Wilton replied.

"I have to go home now," Samuels said.

"Please don't."

"Really, I've got to go," Samuels said.

"Sit beside me and talk," Wilton urged.

"Can't," Samuels answered.

Wilton fumbled with the shoulder bag he carried. He stood up and faced Samuels.

As he did, everything happened at once.

A voice boomed out from the path not more than ten yards away. "Freeze, Wilton. Freeze."

It was Jackson.

The dog broke away and began to race across the lawn.

Six headlights lit up across the lawn and began to move rapidly across the open field. Three police cars in a line.

The lovers on the bench leaped up and raced toward Samuels and Wilton. The lovers beneath the tree did the same. The old woman jumped from her bench and ran toward them, a gun in her hand.

A chubby figure raced after Bernard. Samuels, in an instant, knew the movement. It was Morgan, with another figure, Markham, behind him.

"Oh, God, oh, God," Wilton said. He was crying. "Oh, God," he chanted.

Samuels backed away from him, slowly.

Again Wilton repeated, "Oh, God."

Samuels stared at him, frozen by the moaning sound of Wilton's voice.

Jackson screamed, "Freeze, Wilton. Don't move."

Wilton turned toward Samuels, the gun still in his hand. Jackson fired one shot into the air.

Wilton's face was contorted in torment. He lifted his hand, holding the gun, into the air above his head; he fired into the sky. He squeezed the trigger again and again. It clicked. He had fired his only bullet. The gun fell from his hand; he fell to his knees.

Samuels saw the gun fall to the ground. He moved toward Wilton.

"I am so sorry." Wilton wept. "So very sorry." He stared at Samuels. Samuels moved closer to him and put his arm on Wilton's shoulder. Wilton put his arms around Samuels' legs and sobbed. Lightly Samuels patted him on the back.

They were surrounded. Morgan had the dog by the leash and he and Markham had come back. Jackson had rushed up.

Goldman, in tattered old clothes, shopping bag in one hand, gun in the other, looked at Jackson. "You didn't hit him," he said.

"I wasn't trying to hit him," Jackson said. "I'm glad I didn't have to. I don't think I'm one of your killer cops."

"Shit," Morgan said.

Uniformed police piled out of the squad cars and joined the crowd.

"Our man?" Fahey asked.

"Our man," Jackson said.

A fourth squad car pulled up and a man got out on the run.

"Who are you?" Jackson asked.

"Dr. Weinstein," he said, "his doctor."

Jackson pointed to Wilton.

"Should I have known? Should I have guessed?" Weinstein sighed.

"Don't ask me."

"I'm not."

Weinstein knelt beside Wilton and said, "How are you?"

"Very tired. And alone."

"But alive."

"Irrelevant," Wilton said. "Irrelevant."

Fahey took charge, along with several of his men from the precinct and two delegates from Homicide.

192

"Meet me back at the precinct," he said to Jackson.

"Sure."

Jackson walked toward Samuels, who had moved away from Wilton and was standing with Morgan, Markham and the dog.

"Thanks," Jackson said. "It couldn't have been easy for you. Or you. Or you," he added, nodding toward Morgan and Markham. "Go home now. We'll be talking to you later, to all of you. For now, go home."

"Take the dog," Morgan said.

Jackson grabbed the leash. The dog lunged toward Wilton.

"Easy," Jackson whispered, "easy."

"Maybe we'll see each other again," Samuels said to Jackson. "I mean later, when it's all over."

"Maybe we will," Jackson answered. "But I plan to stay out of this park. Pretty soon it'll be fall and then winter and I've got other things to do. You will too. School and all that."

"I guess you're right," Samuels said. "I hadn't thought about it."

"Well, think about it."

"I will."

"See you soon."

"Later," Morgan said.

"Time to tip," Markham added.

The three boys walked across the lawn, Samuels in the middle with one arm around Morgan and the other around Markham. They headed west, toward the buildings and the lights on Central Park West.

Jackson walked back to where Goldman was standing. "You look terrible. You need a bath," he said.

"Who has time?" Goldman said.

"And get a new suit, please."

"I'm at work. Don't make fun of me. Maybe you should get your ass out of here and back into Mary's bed."

"I can't. I'm at work too. Remember? And I'm not all that sure anymore about Mary."

"Really? You'll have to explain that to me one of these days."

"I will. As soon as I explain it to myself."

They got into one of the squad cars, behind the one carrying Fahey and Wilton and Weinstein. The motor roared and the car moved forward, its roof lights flashing. It made its way south, away from the lawn and toward the precinct house.

"Tell me one thing," Goldman said.

"What?" Jackson asked.

"Why didn't you make a move when Wilton first picked up Samuels? Why did you get into all that running and hiding and waiting?"

"If I move in and he doesn't have the gun with him, our case is weak. I took a chance. If I foul it up, I look for a new line of work."

"Have you been thinking about a new line of work?"

"Yeah, once in a while. But I didn't want to have the decision made for me, not that way."

"So you went for the sure thing?"

"Yeah. I waited and hoped for the best."

"You got it," Goldman said, patting Jackson on the shoulder. "You must be one smart cop. If I were you, I'd stay in this business. There's hope for advancement for you."

"Maybe I am smart. But it wasn't being smart that worked. That poor guy just played out his hand. And we were there. In time. Thank God."

The squad car sped through the park to the precinct house. Jackson got out and went into the station.

Fahey was screaming. "What? Jesus! What?" He was stomping his foot and glaring at one of his uniformed men.

Jackson joined them.

"You know what? You won't believe this. I don't believe this. I don't get one fucking hour off. Not one. I can't stand much more of this," Fahey hollered.

"What?" Jackson asked.

194

"They just found a body in the lake. A guy with a butcher knife in his chest. I don't believe it. Not yet, for Christ's sake. Give me a few minutes. Not yet."

"You'll handle it, Sergeant," Jackson said, barely suppressing a smile. "With your own men. I'm going to fill out all those forms we love so much and get out of here, to something warm to hold and something cool to drink. And then back to my friends in Street Crime."

"Yeah. Go bust some pusher in Queens. Go ahead."

"I sure will," Jackson said.

"And thanks," Fahey said. "Thanks." He had managed a smile.

"You're welcome," Jackson said. "I'll see you in the park when I have a day off."

"You certainly will," Fahey said.

ACKNOWLEDGMENTS

I would like to thank several people for their advice, guidance and information; each one of them enhanced my understanding of life in Central Park, and the behavior of those who frequent it, or might frequent it.

Dr. Lawrence Hatterer and Dr. Myra Hatterer were extremely helpful and generous with their time. Detective Frank Giugliano (Ballistics), Detective Thomas Spratt (Central Park precinct) and Lieutenant Peter Princi (Street Crime Unit) were particularly kind and informative.

I am indebted to Henry Hope Reed and Sophia Duckworth for the excellent reference material in their splendid book, *Central Park: A History and a Guide.*

I would like to thank my son, Paul, for planting the seed of the idea for this novel in my mind. And Owen Laster, my literary agent, adviser and good friend, for his attention and support. Finally I want to express my gratitude to my editor, M. S. Wyeth, Jr., a patient, compassionate and wise man.

D. G.